THE PENGUIN POETS

THE BOOK OF NODS

Jim Carroll was born and grew up in New York City. In addition to his prose and poetry writing, he has an ongoing career as a rock musician and has released three albums for Atlantic Records. Many of the works in *The Book of Nods* have appeared in such publications as *The Paris Review*, *Rolling Stone*, *Transatlantic Review*, and *Big Sky*, while several others have been read by the author on MTV, in the film *Poetry in Motion*, and on the record album *Life Is a Killer*.

The
Book
of
Nods

Jim Carroll

Penguin Books

PENGUIN BOOKS
Viking Penguin Inc., 40 West 23rd Street,
New York, New York 10010, U.S.A.
Penguin Books Ltd, Harmondsworth,
Middlesex, England
Penguin Books Australia Ltd, Ringwood,
Victoria, Australia
Penguin Books Canada Limited, 2801 John Street,
Markham, Ontario, Canada L3R 1B4
Penguin Books (N.Z.) Ltd, 182–190 Wairau Road,
Auckland 10, New Zealand

First published in simultaneous hardcover and paperback
editions by Viking Penguin Inc., 1986
Published simultaneously in Canada

LIBRARY OF CONGRESS CATALOGING IN PUBLICATION DATA
Carroll, Jim.
   The book of nods.
   I. Title.
PS3553.A7644B6   1986   811'.54   85-40623
ISBN 0 14 058.594 4 (pbk.)

Some of the poems in this collection first appeared in
*Big Sky #3, Little Caesar #3, Walker Arts Center Broadside,
Long Shot #2, The Paris Review, Transatlantic Review,*
and *Rolling Stone.*

Printed in the United States of America by
R. R. Donnelley & Sons Company, Harrisonburg, Virginia
Set in Caslon 540

To Rosemary & Ted

Some of these poems were first published in *The Paris Review*, *The Transatlantic Review*, *Rolling Stone*, *Little Caesar*, *Big Sky*, and *Walker Arts Center Broadside*. Others appeared on the records *Life Is a Killer* (Giorno Poetry systems) and *One World Poetry* (Dutch Imports from The World Poetry Festival, Amsterdam), in the film *Poetry in Motion* (director Ron Mann—Canadian Films), and in the video *The Cutting Edge* (M.T.V. and I.R.S. Records).

Special thanks to Susan Friedland

Contents

The Book of Nods

The Book of Nods

Trained Monkey

I'm a trained monkey. You don't see many of us anymore, though the streets of the larger cities were once filled with us. Who is to say why we have nearly passed, like several of my cousin species of the jungle and rain forest, into extinction? Some say we were no more than a fad and like all fads were bound to pass, that it is no longer charming to see us dance as our masters grind out music from an old and far-off country. But I am a living, breathing thing, and find it abusive to be so labeled.

I would have you know that I am part of a prestigious line of trained monkeys. My grandpapa worked in the movies from the time he was taken from his own mother's breast. He was the one who swirled at his master's feet, as he played a mournful dirge in an exquisite dance of foreboding, as Lawrence Tierny (playing the gangster John Dillinger) walked to that final movie with the traitorous woman in red. My own mother appeared often on the stage in what has come to be called the Golden Age of Television, before she was sold by her trainer, a scoundrel and drunkard, to a life in the streets, dancing, as I still dance, for the coins of children and the good working people returning from their lunch breaks. We worked together through my early years . . . oh, truly it was the most wonderful time of my life.

I recall with the greatest detail the way she would lovingly swat me across the head as I scuffled across her path on the pavement, the way she would teach me, with such patience, the secrets of certain acrobatic stunts which some experts would have you believe are inherent characteristics to our species. (Believe me, they are not inherent, but very much acquired skills . . . for example, have you ever seen a relative of mine, among the trees and trellises of his natural jungle environment, do somersaults on the seat of a bicycle as his mama pedals from the chrome guard above the back wheel?) More than any of this, I remember the touch of her small, pink fingers as she groomed me at night, tugging my ear with her tight lips, and, once again, the loving swat, signaling she was finished, that I should sleep.

With Van Gogh

I am sitting on a park bench in the neighborhood where I was raised as a boy. Van Gogh approaches me in the dark, a wide blue gash laid down his luminous cheeks. There are some thin papers folded beneath his arms, secured by a ribbon. He is wearing a cheap iridescent suit, beneath it a yellow polo shirt with the image of two small green alligators copulating sewn on above the pocket. Over his spiked red hair is a felt hat, its wide brim covered with twelve thick candles. They are burning rapidly in the wind and give off the scent of a cathedral. There is no reason I should know who he is, but I do. He tells me he is going down beyond the running track to paint the Harlem River. I ask him to sit awhile and talk with me, and in a crippled fashion he lowers himself beside me on the bench. I notice the famous missing ear and he sees this and anticipates a question—"It was an experience, right?"— and he laughs. We are both laughing. We cannot stop laughing . . . we are bent over with our fists pounding our guts and howling into the wind as it grows. Just then a woman in a dark dress approaches us in tears. Van Gogh looks up to her, as if to ask, "Why are you doing this?" The woman explains that she has come tonight to realize so many contradictions in her life, that her entire life seems a contradiction and that she is unable to bear such a notion and so has been weeping all through the evening and, now, into the night. Van Gogh and I look to each other and slowly build into even greater fits of laughter. He is pointing up at the woman and clutching my knee and his shoulders are bouncing up and down in hysterics. The woman cries harder, as if for her tears to outdo our laughter. Seeing this, Van Gogh rises. Standing before her, he mutters slowly the phrase, "My many contradictions . . . my many contradictions . . ." over and over; then he closes his fist and smashes the woman across the face with incredible force. As the woman, who I see now is quite beautiful, goes down to the pavement, Van Gogh falls back beside me on the bench and looks at me, laughing. Then he looks down at the woman and speaks, "There, now you really have something to cry about!" He looks back over to me, after a moment of silence, and we begin laughing again. I throw my arms around him and lay my head to his shoulders, continuing to laugh until my tears begin to fall down the lapel of his suit, which is glowing from the fluorescent light in the lamppost above us.

A Poet Dies

I.

Those who die in my dreams have taught me well of the
modern world; I have taken from them an everlasting nobility.
And they die always in the past, where the wooden frames of
windows are too thick for my hands to grip. I hold on above
the streets and watch them, unseen from within. A young
poet has died overnight in his chained bed. His face is shaded
blue with sweet asphixiation; his eyes have left their sockets
and roll back and forth across the shivering floorboards, as if
gravity were upset for the absurdity of his death. His lips are
black and thick like a painted whore. The lymph stones are
sinking beneath his throat. It is all too much for the bearded
doctor, who wipes the condensation from his eyeglasses and
draws a stunning white hood from his bag to cover the poet's
head. He hands the certificate of death to the hotel owner and
the chamber girl to sign. I hear the young girl, who alone is
saddened by the beautiful dead man beside her, tell the doctor that she is able to write, but has no name. He takes the
certificate from her trembling hand with impatience and marks
it with an X beneath the hotel owner's signature. A sheet is
raised over the hooded body and the three withdraw from the
room. I can hear the doctor's laughter trailing down the hallway. I look down once more to the floor, where the poet's
eyes have come to rest along a thin dull carpet. They are
fixed on me, blue and clean.

II.

Only for those who die am I naked in my dreams, and because he has died so young, my body outside his window is
flawless and thin. Some men in finely cut suits in the streets
below are upset by this. They scream up to me in German;
they think it is important I know that they are lawyers. And
they send some young boys at play, who thought me an
angel, around the square to bring them the magistrate. I have
no time for them, my eyes are riveted still to the floor. The

dead poet's eyes are signaling me to a table directly beneath the window. I smash the glass with my jade rings and gather up his notebooks lying there. I place them secure on the sill beside me and look back. But the eyes have dissolved, there is nothing left but some shadows of heat rising from the carpet. Somehow the whole room has changed, and the knotted blood throbbing beneath the hood and sheet is stilled. But the lawyers beneath me are screaming louder, now they are flinging small stones and bits of jagged glass. I see blood across my bare ankles, but it does not sing. I'm driven beneath compassion for those of the past; these vile little fiends, with their stiff, perfect hair and their tattooed pricks, have let their poets die unknown in chained beds. Gravity knows the justice of my revenge, and comes to my aid. I dance on the ledge, with the notebooks of a dead poet between my legs. I wrap my naked body in some blinding foil, and the sun scatters off me in thin lines like wires whose heat slits the lawyers' eyes. Some grey fluid runs from the holes. They cup their ring-laden fingers to their faces and moan and stumble to the gutter to turn on their elbows in the scum pools. I balance like a dancer on the edge and piss on each of them eternal syphilis through the slits, before the cure has been given. I tighten the notebooks beneath my arms for my return, and look down. I will have no more from them . . . I am of the future, and my power is great.

Homage to Gerard Manley Hopkins

Passing through customs was a fast and pleasant experience, not at all what I had anticipated. This was, after all, the capital of a land still reverberating from the shockwave of revolution, and my country, though maintaining relations in a formal sense, was spoken of only in the most hostile terms. Its citizens no longer clung blindly to the rail of oblivion without resistance, led by that banished dictator who deposited so many, by his own hand or through those of his agents, into the abyss. Their eyes seemed wide open now; they embraced the revolutionary council as true brothers of their salvation. The exceptions were few, and holed up in the hills near the border. Their only source of weapons and, indeed, of clothing and food came from the covert aid of my own country. So visitors such as myself are viewed at best as intruders and, more likely, as outright enemies. I wondered, then, why I was passed through the customs line with no search of my baggage and a few perfunctory questions. I'd had much more difficulty crossing the border into Canada last winter, when I was made to remove the spare tire from the trunk of my car so that the inspectors might search among the oily rags and check the insulating lining of an ice chest.

It was true I was here as a guest of a government office, at the invitation of the committee for cultural events. I am a writer and translator; I hold an esteemed post in the comparative literature department of a most prestigious university. Still, I was taken back by the remarkable efficiency of the finely dressed men (three, no less) who greeted me immediately upon retrieving my baggage. They guided me quickly to a car whose engine was already open. No sooner had I touched my body to the spacious back seat than we were weaving throughout the crosshatched traffic, whose cars always seem smaller and unfamiliar in foreign places. Looking closer through the open window, however, I realized these were, after all, quite different from any autos I had seen at home or in my many years of travel. Picking up on my curiosity, one of the agents, who was facing me from a jumpseat, explained how all imports had been banned within the last three months, as far as the automobile industry was concerned. "But, of course, you would know all about such affairs," he whispered enigmatically, his face contorted without any apparent effort into what was, literally, a half smile and half sneer, each side opposing the other like a composite photograph. I replied, puzzled and somewhat anxious, that I had no idea what he meant, then hastened to loosen up the atmosphere of these close quarters . . . which seemed to be growing closer still . . . by commenting how amazing the cars looked and what a genuine feat it must have been to produce them. I fell short of expressing my considered opinion of just how terribly ugly these cars were. There were, from what I'd seen, two uniform models, which did, in their defense, offer exactly twice the variety of Hitler's vision for a vehicle to transport citizens of the fatherland. Both models were hideous. One looked like a shoe. The other was larger, shaped in almost the exact proportions of a coffin. Each had wheels smaller in circumference and width than that of a standard motorcycle, which seemed, right there, to be a failing proposition to even a layman's eyes. From the sounds which enclosed us on either side, it was obvious nobody around the drawing board had considered including mufflers in the design. The sound was deafening; the highway more like a lake during a race for those cigar-shaped, monstrous powerboats. Our own vehicle, I suddenly realized, was more like a sailboat, icily quiet, a leftover import from the old days of the new regime, or, more likely, the early days of the old regime. It was, in fact, an old British Daimler, very much in mint operating condition. Why did I rate an anomaly? The cultural people seemed to put a higher estimate on my work than I myself did, even in my wildest frenzy of ego beneath the halfway point of a fifth of Scotch. I looked closer at my companions; it was a questioning stare that went unanswered. None of them looked at all Latino in feature; they all looked quite the same. The car, I noticed, was getting cold. Not cool, but cold. My companions' breathing grew visible. I was breathing too thinly to give off a sign.

Things began to happen quickly then. Both back windows came up at once, powered by a remote up front. It must have been installed specially; this car predated such devices. The windows were darkly tinted. I could see nothing from them but the reflections of the others and myself, so the space grew even smaller. That's when the fellow opposite me, with the same clashing expression, began to speak. The others moved in tighter and leaned forward; the three tracks of icy breath met and mingled between them in a single small cloud which rose to the ceiling and dissolved. "Sir," he asked in the same whispering tone, "are you familiar with the works of a poet of your own language, a poet by the name of Gerard Manley Hopkins?"

"Yes, of course," I answered, amazed at the question. "A fine poet, and a favorite of mine in my undergraduate days. He was a priest, you know."

"Oh, but indeed I do know," the man, his menace growing, replied, "and I am grateful for your candor in this matter."

I had no idea what he was getting at. My candor about what?

Something else . . . his accent was shifting. He had spoken so little, I hadn't noticed at first the false note in his Latino phrasings of English. Now he seemed to have lapsed into a more East European tone: that methodical, Slavic slurring of words punctuated with short, clipped declaratives.

Outside the car the unmuffled engines had ceased, and I could feel that the texture of the road beneath us had changed from asphalt to dirt. We were obviously outside the city, heading deeper into the countryside. Suddenly there was a thudlike sound, and the driver slammed on his brakes. One man got out while the other two seemed to slide into what they considered to be strategic positions. They moved as casually and calmly as two who had drilled such moves many times. No more than half a minute passed before the third man had returned. He explained that we had hit an animal, and we began to move on. He did not elaborate. He did not say what kind of animal. Neither did he mention if it was killed or still alive.

"Did Hopkins write poems about animals?" I was asked by the same man as before.

"I'm afraid I don't know . . ." I hesitated.

"I don't believe he did," he went on. "And I would know. In the last two months I have read all of his works. I have read them in three languages. I have also read all available biographical material. He was not born Catholic, but converted and, ten years later, was ordained. I think he preferred trees to animals, as far as subjects for his poems . . . trees and his God."

"He had a wonderful way of blending the formal with the colloquial," I blurted back, hardly believing I had said it. I was shaking visibly now, not only from the increasing cold within the car, but from a deep anxiety with the realization that these men were neither from the ministry for culture nor, for that matter, from the country we were in.

"You seem to be shaking, sir," he cooed, draping a blanket, which was thin enough to be totally without use, around me. "And may I say that was an astute comment."

"What?"

"What you said about Hopkins . . . the formal language blended with—"

"It was hardly astute," I interrupted, "and may I ask you what the hell is going . . ."

" 'Ah, as the heart grows older,' " he recited, " 'It will come to such sights colder / By and by, nor spare a sigh / And yet you will weep and will know why . . .' "

I stared at him directly. His composure was becoming comical. I was still afraid, yet found myself angry enough to say what I was thinking. "Your game is becoming ludicrous. I refuse to be a part of it. You are obviously some sort of agents from another government. I have no idea what you want from me, but—"

"My recitation, sir." He cut me off once more. "Have you no comment to make? Please indulge me, for it seems it is more likely you who is playing the game."

"I truly don't know what you mean. As for the poem, you added an extra word in the last line. There is only one, 'will' . . . The second one was your own contribution. Also, you left out an entire line: the one next to the last. It goes, 'Though worlds of wanwood leafmeal lie . . .' Are you satisfied? Is your idiot inquiry finished? Will I be handed a grade?"

He said nothing, but knocked on the glass partition twice. The driver deftly spun the car about, and we were again heading back toward the city. "I'm sorry for the inconvenience, sir," he finally spoke, this time in another accent, decidedly British, "but, you know, we had to be certain. I'm sure you understand, though you played the role with amazing conviction . . . certainly much better than our rather melodramatic East Bloc routine. Now, here is the envelope containing the documents. Your plane tickets are included as well. We'll be returning you to the hotel at the airport now. You'll need sleep; your flight leaves early."

The contorted face had relaxed into something else. He was still quite an unattractive man, and I was glad to be rid of him and his companions when they dropped me at the hotel. I burned the envelope without opening it, flushing the ashes down the toilet. Then I slept.

I never contacted anyone from the ministry of culture, and flew out the next morning, glad to miss the conference. One would think such a strange experience would deeply affect my life. It has not. I've forgotten it . . . in any real sense, that is. I will offer one piece of advice, however: Never learn too well the works of a poet, for, somehow, the works of the masters have infiltrated the systems of those who are dangerous and covert. They have turned lines of beauty and love into codes of identification. Security is maintained in the detection of a flawed meter, and messages of coercion and betrayal are delivered in iambics.

Watching the Schoolyard

It is a decade now past my decadence. My beast wears rings and he hides under the shadows of my silent hesitations. Each image is so clear, yet I have no hands to adore the precision. The finest gestures of the air are traced on my eyelids. I see them and they see me, but there is never a reply. No hollow flash when the light withdraws, leaving with it a crevice where the angel signals, only to begin again.

Still, I think I have moved closer to my heart. Sometimes I sit near a window and watch kids at recess in the schoolyard. They are passing around some thin girl's false eye. They inspect it with a magnifying glass which, I assume, one of them has stolen from his father's desk. When I see them finally give it back and run to the fountain to carefully wash their hands and dry them on their starched shirtsleeves, I realize the eye is quite real. As real as each one's nonchalance, walking back to their games. It could have been a jewel.

They gather in a circle and a leather ball is flung toward the sky. Their thin hands hold back the sun from their sight. But for them, in that shadow, something else moves. And suddenly each one is gone. The ball remains, as if poised on a stream of air. Things are beginning to seem like symbols for my losing control. My cat pumps its hind legs twice, and leaps into the mirror. I need someplace to hide. I undo my belt buckle and tie it tight. I hear a train passing over dried-up waters. I watch stunned heat snap the cold wings of birds.

When I withdraw the point and untie my belt, the thin young girl returns. She comes to my open window with her eye in her palm, extending it to me. It could have been a jewel. It's so real. It makes me feel so human. There are tired lines at the edges, thin and magenta like an insect's veins. But I don't want to look at it; I want to hear it. I hold it to my ear. I hear the calm voice of a woman, whispering some words of love and caution. It must be the girl's mother. It is lovely; I look down to her. Morning has never meant so much as her Christian smile, the perfect weight of her small, wet fingers, as light like crushed glass strains through their crevices.

Guitar Voodoo

I awakened in a pool of mild chemical reaction. I stood up
then in the darkness and felt what it was drain slowly from
my ankles and fingertips. It felt like thousands of lesser hands
weaving small flags beneath my skin. The darkness of that
room hummed like a small machine; there was a thin red glow
shining from the walls. Turned and noticed some strips of
fluorescent light outline a doorway. Felt along there for a
switch . . . there was a button, instead, shaped like a V. I
saw I was in a photographer's darkroom. The liquid I had
woken in, now almost totally dissolved across my skin, must
have been some agent used in the developing process. I
searched over myself to check for damaging effects. There
were no burns, apparently, though my veins glowed a
metallic silver. I ran my forearms under some warm water,
but it only seemed to sharpen the effect. I figured I'd come
back to it later. I began to take a look around. I found a
drawer in a metal cabinet with my lover's name on it. I
forced the lock and withdrew the contents, a box of color
slides she had once taken of her ex-husband. There were a
dozen of them, each with the same pose of him leaning naked
against the trunk of a lavender Bentley. They obsessed me
immediately. I emptied them into my jacket pocket and
returned the box to the drawer, leaving it open. Pushed
another V-shaped button and took an eight-seat jet back to
the city.

I never liked this man. I once read in my lover's diary the
methods he used in bed to please her. What I read haunted
me many months; it reached such clarity beneath my eyes
when I lay beside her in the darkness that for sixteen weeks I
could not bring myself to know her skin. It forced her to return to him each Sunday morning, and when I discovered
this, I led her out one evening to the beryllium flats and with
a shovel dug a place for her to rest. When the time came that
I wanted her back, I realized she had many months before
forgotten how to breathe.

I know guitar voodoo. I learned it from a woman with white hair in the hills above Kingston, who all day slit open the crowns of oranges and raised them above her head for the sun to drink. At night, one day each month, she gathered the dry, pale skins in mounds and left them for the full moon to push back beneath the earth. The cycle gave her great powers, and because I one day taught her the proper way to sharpen the blade on her knife, she gave some power to me.

She opened the case of my guitar and placed six fingertips to the pickups beneath the strings. She made a tea from the dried orange skins on her fire, and taught me the way of guitar voodoo. When I got to my apartment with the photographs, I placed them in a plain glass bowl. I lifted from my dresser the porcelain sphere the white-haired mistress had given me one year past. The scent from the thick golden substance inside was sweet and true like a child breathing . . . this was a by-product of what the sun itself had one day left behind for me. With my adrenaline rising, a slow heat turned like a fist beneath my heart. My hands tightened for the power. I poured the substance into the bowl, over the squares of processed celluloid containing his image. When the last drop rolled out, I put down the sphere and, though it served no purpose for the ceremony, I danced one hour before I slept.

By the time I woke next morning the magic was already complete. I shaved to make myself pretty. I went to the living room sofa; I took the slides from the bowl and laid them in two rows of six across the glass tabletop. I raised the bowl to my lips and drank what was left over. Opened the closet door and removed my guitar from its case. Turned the power on with the switch on the amp and hooked the jacks. I shut my eyes as the potion took me over. There were small globes the color of burst capillaries, framed by an uncertain gravity before a white expanse . . . then an image began to focus. I could see, clearly as the sun, the man who was my lover's husband, lying in bed in his home in northern California. He was just waking. Some shadows of morning light hung from the brass bedposts. He was sitting up now beneath a fancy quilt with his eyes fully opened. I took one of the voodoo slides, turned rigid by the potion overnight, and, fingering on the neck of the guitar an "A" chord, ran his naked image across the strings.

I saw the reaction as if standing behind a mirror on his bedroom wall. His body shuddered violently on the bed. He seemed to be pulled a few inches off the mattress until the sound finally quit reverberating inside the amp. The room was left with a hollow ringing within silence, like air inside a nitrous oxide dream. He gripped his convulsing and stopped it. His eyes searched the room for answers. He checked some objects on top of the bookshelves, praying with moving lips they had been knocked over to sustain his hope that there was an earthquake taking place. But nothing was moved. I was delirious with pleasure. I upped the volume of the amp to "8" and ran the voodooed image across the strings windmill style, like Pete Townsend. He was thrown back down across the floorboards, as if by the force of a giant reptile's tail across his neck. I couldn't figure out if the voodoo force worked from outside his body or within . . . more likely both, I imagined. He quivered on his back and implored the ceiling. On his bare chest six lines of blood, thin as guitar strings, opened and pulsed. I looked down and noticed the red draining down my fingers' crevices . . . the magic was transporting his blood to me. I thought a moment to stop it, but it was out of my control. I slammed into another "G" chord. I saw a woman run into his room and gape in astonishment. When I saw her hands clapped tight across her ears, I realized he was *screaming out* guitar chords from deep inside his lungs, with the same volume produced by my guitar and amp. His larynx about to shatter like a crystal goblet.

More chords . . . he slammed against four walls. He was weakening; my power was growing stronger. His fingers clutched his throat for the pain each uncontrolled shriek was causing. The veins along his forearms were throbbing and choking each other like killer vines. The woman bolted from the room, signing herself with the cross. I realized it was beginning to do him in . . . the building tension of the strings in "E" forced the lines of blood across his chest to spurt like steam from split valves. And it was bringing sounds from within him which human tissue was incapable of bearing. I slapped my hand across the pickups to snuff the sound. I wiped the sweat and blood from the glass tabletop and leaned over to switch off the power in the amp. There was a last image of his body dropping limp and unconscious to the stunned floorboards of his room. I opened my eyes. I undid my belt buckle. And slept.

My Father's Vacation

I have distilled the natural world into a clear clean liquid, so I no longer need to think about it. When I'm there I am contained on all sides by water, what I move through cannot touch me. And the air I breathe is within my veins, as the fire there creates its own wind, on the rush. I don't run, I barely walk before I reach my destination. It's all just so much insulation . . . when the first bombs are whistling overhead, men will be frantic searching for a means to keep out death from their walls. They'll have to rediscover dirt. Junkies have it now, this inscrutable facade. Nothing and no one unasked for gets through the door.

The fact that it's all dropping down the big tube is so much melodrama to me. The reports nightly on the evening news, with their eager visuals of the planet unraveling, might as well be reruns of *Green Acres* to me. I no longer concern myself with cancer. I watch reactors erected through a glass screen in living color. How could it be possible they are just up the Hudson River, no more than an hour's drive away? When my father's vacation came around each summer, when I was a kid, we'd drive an hour in that very direction to swim in a pool with fourteen diving boards. And what if it is there? What if it's somewhere else, on all sides, as they say "Going up?" in the trade? I watch it in color . . . to be honest, I can't even say I'm oblivious to the real *beauty* of processed uranium, to the light blue glow of fissionable rods under water. I imagine it emits a pretty hum, like the reverberation deaf children hear when a tuning fork is placed against their earbones. Besides, I haven't left my room since I fell in love with guns. How can one who hasn't opened his door in three weeks fear anything?

Quality

The man that came by yesterday said our bees were the biggest he had ever seen in this county. "And the result is better quality," I added proudly, pouring the sweet honey into his tea for him to taste. My wife hands me our daughter and I place her across my knee. She does her little trick of turning her head 360 degrees on her shoulders, then giggles with restraint. She, too, is proud. This has all happened in less than two years, in fact, and before that I knew nothing about the small creatures and the manner in which they created the thick, pleasing liquid. The first time I was stung put an end to my last anxiety, and now I accept an occasional sting with a patient, knowledgeable tolerance. They are for the most part so unexpectedly well behaved, and it is only the passing of the jeeps and tanks through the mountain road leading to Camp Davidson that at times upsets them, irritates and leaves them the worse for a short while in the way of production. We couldn't have chosen a more exciting crop and, judging from the miracles it works on our breakfast toast, a more rewarding one either.

Post Office

I.

I have to go out looking for the dog. I hear his curved whine coming from the wooded area down near the pumping station. I knew before I had arrived that the children of the farm workers had once more hung him from the wire drawn between the trees. I cut him loose with some flat broken glass. He is unharmed but shaking . . . he has been dreaming again of rising from the waters. His dreams keep him safe. He has taught me much about it.

I let him follow without the leash. I must make it to the post office before the siren signals noon. I run beside the highway but there is no room to get to the other side, so I hold my rings up to the sun to blind the drivers' eyes. When the traffic is still, I lower my hands and pass through. I arrive before the siren through the post office doors . . . yet the siren has been broken, some jealous women explain, and I am far too late.

II.

Today I leave the dog on the wire. His dreams will keep him safe. He dreams of the ocean; he wants to move forever without sleep, like the shark. So I reach the post office on time. I pass through the corridor and come to the box they have given me. Beside it, a beautiful doll is sleeping without air. In a corner further down, an old man in a coat which touches the floor has his eye on me. He knows I am a thief, and makes sure I take nothing that is not my own. But my patience is flawless, and I know someday he will be reassigned. Then I will steal this woman, and hang her, with the dog, from the wire. Exposed to the silver air, she will glitter. I have been in love with her since I came to this town. I turn the combination to my box, but there is nothing inside.

III.

I have been here too long. The doll is gone. The man in the long coat has taken her place. The dog is dead. He stopped dreaming and drowned on the wire. I had a card in the mail this morning, the same as each day this week. It is a faded blue and white, like Giotto's sky, emblazoned with pure gold leaf. It reads, "Our Lady of the Immaculate Conception would like to invite you to a meeting with your assassin." I laughed until the man behind the glass began to awaken. Without the dog, I can take or leave it.

The Ice Capades

It is deep winter, I am sitting on a dead tree with my guardian, staring down across the pearly blue ice on the pond. Some guitar chords, like claws from a distant balcony, have scratched in the ice the figures of popes, centuries old. They are dressed so neatly, in gold iridescent suits. The crowns they wear are not the crowns of Peter, but of a leader of some bellicose Moorish tribe. I write some words on flat white hair and glide it across the frozen surface like crushed lilies. Darkness curves over the project roofs and draws lines across the thousand pious faces. The ashes from burnt incense have dulled the reflections along the edges of the pond. Some young boys in liturgical gowns are lighting huge candles set in mounts of gold and lapis. Neither my guardian or I are in any way awed by what is taking place. I once fell through this ice. I know what it can do.

My guardian's dog comes to my hand to feed. Then he takes up the razor between his teeth and glides across the skull of our holy fathers to free the stranded insects. One named Leo climbs the steps of a makeshift pulpit. As he begins to speak, a bright orange scum flows down from the drains above his frozen teeth. It flows down the pulpit steps like gasoline, until a candle slips from the hands of an altar boy as he signs himself with the cross. And flames rise to chase the screams across frozen water.

"The Academy of the Future Is Opening Its Doors . . ."

—John Ashbery

On the nod it was five-thirty and the minutes rushed beyond their standard progression, so that each doubled . . . and what was left doubled again. Anyone knows that if you take a penny and double it daily, one to two to four to eight to sixteen, etc. . . . within a month that man would be a millionaire. When time begins to work this way, as it seems to more and more with each nod these days, the results are devastating.

So it was horrible. The Academy was offering a pot-luck dinner in my honor, and my date and I were already terribly late. To make matters worse, I brought the salad but realized on exiting the cab, under the Plaza's heated veranda, I had forgotten our special dressing . . . (paregoric, sesame oil, and crushed lentils). My date gets upset when I talk about it.

You would think that was enough blundering for one day, no matter how time was moving. But I couldn't resist the sky, and my head began to rise. Then, with a slow rush, my lips began to bleed. All over the salad it flowed, and an equal amount on my formal wear.

Now the Academy chairman has appeared through revolving doors. He walked down lucite steps to take my hand. It was the only time I could recall both his hands being empty. He took me aside and whispered into my mouth, his tongue pressed to mine, "You had better go back, we can always do this again some other time."

I thanked him for his consideration and slid back into the cab, exposing thigh-high boots beneath my robe. The chairman deftly ascended the stairs, two by two. He handed the teakwood bowl to the startled doorman, who licked traces of blood from the salad.

Parting the Reeds

I.

I lie drugged along the banks of the Nile. The tall reeds are like fingers, signaling me to the pleasures of death by water. I pass into the tide. I straddle an ancient crocodile and, with the spikes upon my tongue, lick the soft green algae of one hundred years from its neck. He takes me under, the light there is blue as the ceiling of a Cuban church.

II.

My chest has been slashed in lines thin as razors, by wires of light from the summit of a pyramid. I lie twisting on a slab of stone darkened by moss and the shadows of evening. A young boy in pillbox hat comes and pads my wounds with mud from the Nile. He wears no shirt, the flesh across his belly is scarred and stretched. He tells me of the time he climbed to the eye of Cheops and was drenched by tears of acid and scented oil. I notice an old man to his right, drinking from the shoreline through a hollow reed. His eyes are red and white, and twice the size of the boy's or mine. As he moves toward us, I see he is blind. The boy leans to me and whispers of a time the old man was led away by a ruler for words he had written in his youth. They removed his eyes with prongs in the desert and fed them to some pitted snakes. Then he was led to the river, to the place we now stand over, and he was given the eyes of a crocodile. From that day, he turns to this very place each evening and plays music through an instrument whose voice resembled the sound of an ocarina.

The Lakes of Sligo

She was speaking into the telephone in the cracked glass booth across the street from The Lakes of Sligo saloon, down the block from Needle Park. She fingered more and more dimes through the tubes and they slid until my bell began to ring. I was lying in bed with a burnt spoon messing the sheets. And there was water spilling. The idea of heaven seemed a bit too simple . . . then again, there was no reason it shouldn't be just that. If the stars are milked. If the angels' bones are hard and sharp like badly split diamonds. She is speaking now on the telephone, asking for more time. I don't have a phone. I hear her speaking nonetheless. And I see each word as if they were colors from the phantom's lips. Out the window I watch a taxi passing by a woman with a shiny cane on Broadway. Six Temple elders feed the single pigeon the dried wafer in islands between the traffic. Another try with the needle through the fungus like a nightshade mushroom on my thigh. There is some mean gravity waiting beneath that flesh. Nothing is happening. At all.

So I cannot answer it . . . you see, I have no phone. I've tried to convince you. I want you to know I can feel it, cruising down my spine. Like the sharp blue light of wheels beneath the earth. Cannot answer. Cannot win. Always and only just sit and watch.

She knows this. She expects no reply. She says she wants to take the ride, but she needs to find herself. She knows I watch out for her. And she knows I'm watching now. She opens the door of the booth with flair, and sinks her eyes to each soft breast, where she unzips the shield and folds it open. So I might see the blue crevice surrounding her nipples, which rise like infant fingers out of clean ice.

Lenses

Each night she comes to me, places the glass from her eyes into a small green box with mirrors. Music down the living darkness begins. Some low-eyed Rastafarians, fingers sharp and gleaming as the knives inside suns, enter the room in lines. They lay hands like machetes across steel drums and chant the deep orange. There is power there is sweetness there is parallel light.

Within her heat, the glass above the bed turns to violent water and I lift her up the moment before the drowning. I set her loose. I pull her back again. No one knows none of them could ever know. It is not for learning or love, these dreams and their actions. It is our way of surviving.

When it is finished, the chanters throw their headdress into the hollow flux. They take up flutes and strings to give music to exhaustion. The speed of each dream can turn on me then under these rapid lids. The symbols of elements pass by me; it is only some clever women in disguise. Their bones are so sharp; they can break through their own excuses. And we sleep when the music is done, with our wrists resting in the holes their children have dug beside us in the sand.

A Beach Landing

Pictures in a thick time-stained sky . . . a ship moving out.
All the sailors are plenty happy, wide grafted faces winking to
the little galley helper. Even on the shore, none of the wives
crying, they're all just slapping backs and swinging to and fro
tweed baskets filled with everything needed to get well quick.
There's a few Indians under shawls on the nod across a thin
patch of beach. Sailor's wife offers Indian a basket: "No
thanks, just nod good enough." Back on the ship, the crew
still smiling. A rack of pork meat out drying. It's a nice ship,
gold knobs on every door. The cargo they will carry is one of
candles and books, and the crew is enthused . . . they will
read all night. But one sailor looks horrible. "All the others
are happy," he speaks, "but I feel hideous." He goes to the
captain, sitting with his hand dangling across the chair's arm,
like Christ . . . or Sherlock Holmes. Certainly a wise pos-
ture . . . a wise man. And he *is* Christ-like. He signals the
sick sailor to the door; the sad man is lowered in a leather har-
ness into a small rowboat and taken back to shore, the second
year in a row this has happened.

Zeno's Final Paradox

I am resting on the glimmering salt flats, sewing emblems on
my endurance. There is a malignant smoke pouring from the
summits of distant mountains; shreds of warm asbestos settle
across my chest. I follow the flight of a single vulture into a
stranded cloud. My eyes are dry and cracked, like this desert
surface surrounding me on all sides with no end within my vision. An old Greek man named Zeno pulls up on a rocket
sled and lectures me on motion. The first step, he insists, can
never be taken . . . for half the distance will always remain
ahead. Neither time, speed, nor unyielding endurance can
make a difference. At each step of its ascent and fall, the
arrow in flight is dead . . . it does not move, but rests contin-
uously in progressing intervals . . . like the stars and planets
seen through some shuttering eye. "Even as it pierces the target at point center it is an illusion," he goes on, "the target
itself is a lie, and neither you nor I shall ever leave this
place."

Paraguay

It is all too white again. The sun has bars across its lids; the light reaches us in shafts. Numbers form across our breakfast. Someone speaks of a place where all the women are called "Madonna."

Keats is there at the table, drinking coffee and dark pine methadone. He won't give me a taste, it's bad because I oversleep a lot and miss the hours at the clinic. I'm in the bathroom disassembling the pipes. My wrists are strong in dreams, there is no need for tools. Keats speaks to me through the closed door, "There is no escape, you try to figure out what is inside and, with that knowledge, move around it. The birds, after all, do not touch earth until felled by disease." The last line, the one about the birds, sounded bogus to me . . . so I open the door to check. It's not Keats after all, it's my little sister and her tape recorder again. She smiles sinisterly and raises her dress to me. I return to the pipes, they are clean now and must be put back.

I fall asleep there on the blue carpet. It's Paraguay. A country where the trestles are rising and the birds pass through quickly. Along the countryside, the landscape is covered with bloodstained sombreros. The fat workers sing along with the music from speakers nailed to a white sky. They gather stones in burlap shawls and fling them like brown eyes at the dictator passing through the gates of the palace when the bridge is lowered at dawn and the sun drowns the voices of agriscientists returning to draw blood on the cattle before their children wake. But they are wakened nonetheless, with their bellies stretched like drums, sweet with poverty and infant grace. They know by the volume of the guns that I have just landed on their shores.

The Safe Corridor

I am walking along Eighth Street on my way to the East
River; there are things floating by there I want to watch. I can
hear the convicts pacing with superb dignity along the cat-
walks beneath these thin sidewalks. They work for the system
on commission, scraping jumpers from the tracks. Soon their
steel shoes will be silent with the changing of the guard.
Some take the time for prayer, using chains like rosary. Some
listen for the gathering of whores, when they masturbate their
partners to the clicking of their false eyelashes. There is a lucite brick through which one can watch them; in front of the
shop selling masks from Africa. It is not advised, however; the
penalty is severe for non-officials. For their part the convicts
are never changed, they sleep leaning against the rail, like
horses. It seems cruel to some, but the facts remain . . . the
men themselves would have it no other way. The suicide ex-
change rate rises steadily, and, as was mentioned, they work
on commission.

As I reach Broadway and Eighth I realize I will get no further on foot. When evening comes, the next block, the one
leading to Astor Place and the East Side, is impassable, ravaged by the gamma wind from the beryllium plants flanking
both sides. They are each forty flights, and though darkness
has not fallen, there is no light left through this narrow passage. On weekend nights, some school kids try to beat the
wind and blackness on a bet . . . none make it through without two layers of skin left behind. So I enter, enter the booth
at the entrance to the safe corridor and hand the attendant my
card.

He cautions me that the corridor is sealed off from the general public for the day because of a system inspection in prep-
aration for some dignitaries from the Middle East tomorrow. If
it's real important, he assures me, I can be issued a white suit
for passage and try to hitch a ride through on an authorized
vehicle. I decide to settle for his offer, and he runs my card
beneath a thin beam and hands it back. He unzippers the
back of a white suit, not unlike something worn at my academy while training for post-meltdown relief, and helps me

into it. When I'm completely fastened, he puts me through a detection ring and runs down the procedure for hitching passage. I wait on the southwest corner of Broadway and stick out my hand, exposing the transit badge I was issued. Before long, a flatbed truck with two fourteen-foot lead screens rising on both sides pulls up at the curb next to me. An old man is driving; he puts out his hand and I extend the badge for his edification. He sees that all is in order and gestures silently for me to board myself on the flatbed in back. As I climb on I notice an old black man already crouched in the corner, his back against the cab. I fasten myself with a strap beside him and the driver pulls out. As we move into the black wind I see the whores taunting the convicts beneath them through the lucite brick. One with huge breasts stands over it with her legs spread wide, so those under her might see.

Rimbaud Scenes

Rimbaud's Tooth Ache

Arthur had waited too long. Even the blue light of opium no
longer countered the pain. His teeth throbbed with it, like
the veins of a young soldier in the heat of a battle already
lost. He wailed alone at night in the painter's loft, until the
old man living one flight up, a pedant with dry blood between
the many crevices in his forehead, knocked on the door and
inquired what the trouble might be. Arthur, too tired to shield
himself behind his usual wit and insolence, made a gesture toward the swollen jaw, and the old man insisted he accompany
the youth to a dentist he had known to be "quite reliable and
competent," and who had offices nearby. He would be by to
call on him following breakfast next morning, and, if Arthur
had no money to cover the expense, he insisted on arranging
payment himself with the dentist, who, he added, was a long-
time friend and an understanding sort.

Rimbaud could not deny the comfort he felt in the idea
that at this same time tomorrow the ache would be gone, yet
he could not help but lie back on the bed and regard the old
man as a fool. For the wailing that brought this neighbor to
his door had little to do with the pain upon his teeth. He
wailed for a young girl who sat that day by the fountain he
passed daily as he walked. Her dress was trimmed with lace,
white as the veils of children in processions back home. How
the spray from the fountain pressed the lines of sun deeper
and deeper into her hair until the light remained beyond the
cursed evening! "How will I ever dream again in daylight,"
he thought, "when I know she walks the streets of this city,
and breathes the air?" The darkness was already full as she
rose to go her way, and as she passed the bench where the
poet had set himself, he drew a ragged notebook from his vest
with great haste and pretended to read from its pages, which
were empty. And she passed right by, the last drops of light
sliding through the hair across her shoulders. At his feet. His
fingers quivered with an unbearable longing. To touch. This

was the source of the pain which the old man heard this night, sounding through the floor beneath him.

Rimbaud Sees the Dentist

As he had promised, the old man knocked at Arthur's door early that morning. Rimbaud was ready, and together they passed down into the fresh blocks of sunlight on the sidewalks. Rimbaud was neatly dressed, though his frail black tie, which was more like the lace of a boot, could not conceal the lines of dirt along his collar.

"You should hold no fear of the pain one often takes for granted on the way to the dentist," the old man explained, "for this particular one has lately been experimenting with a strange new form of gas, called nitrous oxide, which is, to all reports, quite successful in eliminating such discomfort."

Rimbaud nodded to that, though, as things were, he was rather looking forward to an experience which involved the purging of one form of pain by means of another, even greater, pain. By the time they had reached the office, however, and the old man had made payment and Arthur had been seated in a chair not unlike that of a barber, he had grown curious about this new gas, and asked the dentist if he might inhale some as part of his treatment. The dentist, who was fat, with a stale yellow beard, was delighted this young man knew of his innovation, and he began to attach, somewhat clumsily, a black mask shaped like a cup over the poet's mouth and nose. A long rubber tube ran from the mask to a cylinder placed behind the chair. He turned a knob on the mouth of the cylinder, readjusted the mask, patted the young man's shoulder and told him to relax, that he would return in a short time. "There is no time to speak of that is short," Arthur was mumbling. "And there is a tiny German whose clothing is in flames running in circles along the back of my jaw." The dentist chortled and walked through the door to his outer office; he knew the drug was already at work. The old man had told him his young patient made claims to writing poems, and now he would allow some time to pass before he began extracting teeth, and he would let the poet dream.

So Rimbaud dreamt the nitrous dreams. Of women with black skin whose lips were like drums. Of rodents sealed in kegs of blue water. Of lightning shaped like freight trains passing vertically through the branches of a tree. Whose leaves were knives falling to the earth and standing upright. There was a speed in these visions, each dissolved to the next with thin wheels in flame dropping from the sky. And there were words painted in many colors across the foreheads of women whose arms linked like a chain. The smell of burning rubber clung with thorny fingers to the ceiling of his skull.

Waking in a Painter's Loft in Paris

He woke and arranged the night's dreams across the floor like playing cards. The flowers at bedside were strong with the scent of valerian and scum. Feeling through his pants, draped across the arm of a plain wood chair, searching for his pouch of tobacco, Rimbaud felt the locket he had carried about for years now in his hip pocket, presented to him by Izambard's saintly aunts as he left them weeping at the staircase that last visit . . . giving in to the demands of his mother's anguished communication. He treasured the locket as he treasured these sisters, not as the poet but as the youthful wanderer. Yet he kept it concealed:

"I want my hands and neck to be free and clear," he had told a school friend years before, "no crucifixes and no rings, for my hands are decorated well enough by the coarse lines of blood which run through them, sometimes forming vowels in silver across my palms when the moon is right. . . ."

Rimbaud Running Guns

The representatives of the chieftain stride abreast through the doors of the Great Bear Inn. The bronze stars inlaid across their teeth caused men in corner booths to fumble for their notebooks. The seams of their robes brushed lightly across the sawdust. Their black skin could do nothing less than radiate the half-darkness of their surroundings . . . they knew no man in Marseilles wore upon his back a finer quality of silk.

Forming their words by the thrashing of the tongue against inflated jaws, they beat out the sounds:

"Rimbaud? We seek Rimbaud."

They sought in unison. They were four in number, one for each season, I would imagine, for the numbers of poetry would follow Jean-Arthur with the same intensity with which he sought to escape it.

"Speaking," summoned the poet, emptying a corncob pipe across the foot of a very fat man. He was with beard, now, less than a month . . . still, beneath it his skin remained the textured white of the gloves worn that day of first Communion. His eyes were his eyes only.

Rimbaud rose from a round table; playing cards tumbled from his sleeve. If it were the West, he would need to summon lightning from his hip. Here, in fact, painters with thick fingers laughed and coughed beer along the floorboards. The chieftain's main man, whom the others referred to as "Sire Ambassador," spoke in the same manner . . . that of a drum:

"We seek 43 gross rifle, the same, if you please, as the last; many, many bullets . . . whatever amount our bearers might safely transport; 16 Russian mortar launchers . . . or, as I suspect you prefer, a like number of American bazookas; and, finally, yet in the sacred eyes of our great Chieftain, most important of all these things, a Gatling gun."

"This shall be without difficulty," the poet replied. "I like the sound of that immensely, don't you?"

"What sound is that you refer, sir?" puzzled the black man.

"Gatling gun, dear Sire Ambassador," opined Jean-Arthur.

"Yes, it is quite lovely, this sound . . . it is not unlike 'Gathering grain' . . . no?"

35

Rimbaud Pays Homage to Saint Helena

His lips climbed the arc of Verlaine's back with such purity of breath, he whistled "Ave Maria" against the thorny spine. With this curling innocence revealed, he dared overturn the master and fixed his eyes with pagan blessing on the gold inlay of a crucifix chained to Verlaine's airy breast. He lent his thumbs to a scarred nipple, caressing there with his need for pain, and withdrew. He descended his lips and kissed the feet of the jade Christ figure and fingered the cross with the curiosity of a child inspecting gears beneath the skirt of a mechanical ballerina. Under the intensity of this tunneled scrutiny, Verlaine felt a sharp discomfort in his bowels. He wanted to excuse himself to the end of the hallway but under these eyes he was rightly pinned. It covered him without warning and suffocated like a deadly pillow. Rimbaud turned about the object with stained forefingers and undid a latch in back of the cross with his fingernails, thin and dangerously long.

It opened to reveal resting on a strip of liturgical velvet a fragment of soft wood, the size of a starving insect. He sought Verlaine's eyes:

"What, then, is this sliver of wood, which rests upon such fine velvet?"

"It is a fragment of the true cross on which died the Savior Jesus Christ, while wept beneath him a whore named Magdalene on the Mountain of the Skull."

Rimbaud had already known exactly what it was, and he was amused by the prosaics of his companion's reply. He knew also that this cross, with its gaudy filigree, must surely be a gift from Verlaine's wife, whom he despised with a flowing passion. Yet his eyes swelled, for the myth of his childhood was a breath away. They sank in that moment to his lover's chest, where Verlaine could feel the quivering of lips. Suddenly, like a piston, with a muffled speed, he drew up with his teeth the sacred sliver from its antique bed, as a child would remove a rose thorn from his fingertip. Verlaine bolted

straight up on the bed, the force knocked candles to the floorboards and hot wax sought the crevices. Already Jean-Arthur
had leapt to the corner of the room, striking poses he had
learned from bearded soldiers at the Commune barracks. And
he swallowed the molding relic . . . and inhaled, deeply and
seven times, the air available to him.

Verlaine leaned in disarray from the edge of the bed, his
fists digging between tight thighs, the crucifix around his neck
open. No question he did not notice the patch of velvet beneath him on the throw rug. His tongue locked by his teeth
for silence. Rimbaud spoke:

"Now the history of Christ's death rests in my body, and
will pass through by morning! Tell me, what poison could be
more exquisite?"

Confederate Lake

She leans toward the left, her long hair in the oval mirror a
cameo that crawls. She thinks someone's watching; she wonders who she will be tonight. The brush in her hand combs
her thigh as her eyes grow large, and she hears a breeze
through the far trees, through their last leaves.

A taste, slow and dry, of fear winds itself between her
teeth, flawed by gaps, and settles casually beneath her
tongue.

The brush lands silent on the rug as the hand freezes,
opened and low. And the reflection turns to clear blue air before the mist rolls through. A breeze builds inside her ears.
She hears the sound of a tree falling on the still water of a
lake. She wonders which lake. She feels a sudden panic,
afraid it was Confederate Lake. Along Confederate Lake
there was only a single tree. It was huge and older than her
oldest relative . . . even those ones she barely remembered,
who were now dead. She thought of this lake as some others
remember a dog, or cat. It served her childhood summers.
The thickest branch reached from the sloped shore directly
out over the water, the clean water of innocence and clear
memory. From this branch her uncle had hung a hairy,
braided rope. They swung from the slope with a running
start, swallowing deep the danger of such still summer air.
Out they flew to the peak, more and more breathless, hanging
then in that moment of timelessness. They let go; the water
climbed toward them. They would stay late every day, until
the water turned cold for evening and they wrapped themselves in blankets between jumps, their teeth clicking in unison. Killing time by picking the shells of cicadas from the
huge trunk . . . much like the shell she left in the mirror
now, as she walked hurriedly through the door to use the telephone in the next room.

One Hundred Years of Boredom

There is a strange glow in the newborn's eyes, and the lips, though soft, seem the shade and texture of poached salmon. They smile and sneer, shifting sides in a single bent gesture. I think of the monoliths of Easter Island. The child turns its gaze on me as if it was not pleased with the looseness of connections within my thought. Surely I am exaggerating matters to myself . . . but now a few more new mothers enter the house to wish my sister well, united by the shrewdness of their fertility. The phone is not working. You probably knew that as well as I.

At least the road is sealed by the junta's men. It's the first thing they've done in years that I fully agree with. But I suddenly remember that the mail boat will be due to enter the harbor within an hour. I round up some couples from their siesta embrace and lead them to the water. There we set off the entrance to the harbor, with one long line of cheap barrels as a blockade, strung together by all the rope we could salvage from the general store. Looking down at it from the cliff now, it resembles the giant rosary of a simple monk. Surely this is a good sign. We are a simple people; we trust in God. And may we always have the faith to do so!

Silent Money

Long a diplomat of an illusion in decay, a devotee of a mimicry without source, he curls up lazily on the corner, like the tongue of a cat, and rails at each passerby with non-sequiturs, his hand extended only enough to make it difficult to reach. He likes the tentative shuffle.

He's sold every face he owns, and their shadows. Sometimes he bargains, "I'll die for your sins, if you will live for mine."

Yesterday, he arrived earlier than usual to find an ecologist with a stained beard in his spot. The man was bent over in a consumptive cough, holding a sandwich board which said, NOW OUR EARTH IS SHAPED / IN THE CHARACTER OF MAN. He didn't get what it meant. He screamed at him and threatened him if he didn't leave his area at once: ". . . or I'll kick your ass to the magic mountain." He was not dumb. In a past he barely recalled, he had read many books.

Sometimes, though rarely, he would engage me in a lucid conversation, letting loose the character he played. I remember in particular a dream he described. "I was right here, as I am in all my dreams (which I find horrible), and a woman . . . an old, bothersome woman, like the ones with the rags, shopping bags and lime-green shoes . . . asks me the time. I scream at her to go away . . . I mean, doesn't she see I have no watch? And the clock on the left spire of the office building across the square is broken. It *did* work once, you know . . . when did you first come around? Forget it. Listen. I'm screaming, and suddenly I am vomiting the hands of a clock . . . one about the size of a, say, kitchen clock, though they were in roman numerals, the numbers that followed the hands . . . and they were coated with that uranium stuff, like the wristwatches that glow in the dark. And the woman waits until it's all up and says, 'That's because you have eaten so much time.' Dumb shit dream, huh? I thought that was a good last line though, didn't you? Maybe you could write about it. It probably wouldn't be as good written down though. At least, that's been my experience. Oh, yes, *I've* tried writing myself . . . why do you think I always dream about this place. Always. I could be dreaming now."

What was strange about what he said was the part about me writing it down, since I'm certain I never told him I was a writer. He assumed other things correctly as well. It was that intuition of a beggar. Lazy as he was, he had the touch that was needed.

And that included knowing when a place was stripped barren. He left two days ago. All he said was he was trying, "Another cosmopolitan area." The spare change was getting sparse. It was all coin . . . thin coin. "A beggar hates loud money," he always said. "There is no sound as pretty as the sound of silent money."

Scouting

It's spring training for the major league ball clubs. Some people think I'm a big deal, working as I do for the big city team, but the fact is I'm small-time. I hang around the sandlots and playgrounds, which seem fewer and fewer each year as the cities themselves shrink, looking for a "viable commodity," as they are called in this new age. "Good prospect" was a term that used to suffice. The colleges, once a wasteland for real talent, are now the only consistent source of prime commodities. It's true, I do, even these days, find some kid who turns out to be the real thing . . . some kid with a cheap glove, a uniform whose top mismatches its bottom, on some playing field in the Bronx, with grass unmowed for three seasons, and basepaths of broken bottles of domestic beer. I try not to live in the past, but I can't deny the system was better in those days. The playing fields more charged with that strange energy of cool ambition and recklessness. Yes, it is more of a thrill to find a future star among the rubble, miles away from the flawlessly groomed diamonds of the campuses out west, where the uniforms fit as tight and suggestively as the leather and denim of a country singer . . . to reach back into the past and find that kid whose talent transcends all odds, even the whims of nostalgia I tie onto him, and watch him make it all real. It's true I get very little for my discoveries. The club throws me a bonus, which translates, if my pig Latin is correct, into being tossed a bone. *Bone* being *bonus,* the plural being *boni.* Indulge me this whimsy. I am old, and age breeds digression. Besides, with the money comes, each spring as now, a ticket by air to this place in the sun, where the young players treat me with a respect I am hardly worthy of, and even the oldest of the great veterans find time to come into the stands where I sit, and shake my hand and ask about the well-being of myself and my family.

Five Irresponsible Students of Zen

Five irresponsible zen students sit at the thick wood table for dinner. They are all related, and each is devoted to poetry. When they speak of zen, they are all in agreement. This is pleasant and understandable, for they each share the same teacher, and they believe him the greatest master in the city. When they speak of poetry, however, great disputes often arise, as each is devoted to the works of a different master. Their own poetry is mediocre. As students of zen, they are brilliant, though, as I have noted, quite irresponsible. Each has found what their teacher calls "the perverse hole" within their own deep powers of meditation. The master has noticed this with alarm, and, on more than one occasion, has warned the brothers of its dangers. He has warned them individually and, just that afternoon, gathered them together after the lesson and, again, reproached their method. They were laughing about just this as they sat at table, awaiting food.

Their mother, who is really their aunt, old and charmingly bent, serves them the special meal she has prepared: steamed rice cakes, shark tongue, and peacock eyes. There is much rice wine. They are celebrating the end of their formal training. Not used to the effects of saki, and having each toasted their teacher, they are soon quite drunk.

Thoughtlessly, they *become* the table. The room is quiet for a moment, then they release themselves. They laugh, spilling food from their mouths. They shake their heads violently, as if they had just emerged from a long time underwater.

Each quotes a haiku to honor the day, and another to pay homage to their teacher. They address their poem to an empty place set for their master. This is not formal tradition, but simply a drunken notion arrived at a moment before. Then, with a flawless lack of aim, they each balance a peacock eye on the tip of the chopstick. Held up to the last vestiges of day's light, the eyes are an iridescent blue and green. "Why, it is like the ring that converges in the center of the peacock's own feathers!" one notes. The others grunt. They are growing dizzy and numb. The peacock eyes spill off the

43

sticks and roll across the mat. A cat appears from the garden and swats one savagely with its paw.

They decide to *become* the table again, and *become* the meal that lies, finished, across the table. Again, in their meditation, the sound of water rushing. But now the saki misleads their focus and the water's current grows . . . a knot in the table left by a worm . . . a ravaging whirlpool. The taste is salty, not sweet like a still pond. From the kitchen the aunt, a different aunt, hears a violent knocking of wood. As she enters the empty room, the cat bolts into the garden. She lifts the bowls as she calls out their names.

The Buddha Reveals Himself

That day when the Buddha first spoke at the deer park at Varanese some unknown merchant died in the exact place where, earlier that morning, a herdsman—who also was unidentified, though a younger man than the merchant—had died. Both died by the same means, drowning, within the same current, near an anvil-shaped rock some one hundred fifty yards off the banks of the River Indus, crossing on a raft secured by faulty knots (though neither raft was, as some had first suspected, the work of the same craftsman).

There was, apparently, a single difference between these tragedies. The herdsman left a legacy; the merchant did not. The herdsman's pig, it seems, was somehow rescued to the shore. The merchant's silver and jade, however, sank immediately to the dank, swirling bottom.

Me, Myself, and I

I was born in a pool. They made my mother stand. Gravity was unsure of me from the start; as I slipped from the womb I did not fall, but rose into the sky and over the cities. It was night, and the clouds were restless. I have been this way ever since. When I finally came down . . . when I was released after days, no one left their buildings for weeks. I sought out the streets near the filthiest markets for food, and their pure silence was embedded in me. With the first sound of footsteps, I took to hiding behind the side altars of churches. I worshiped there . . . not for God, but for silence. It was gone; its pureness broken by the shifting of beads, a candle lit loudly by arthritic fingers. I moved always down deeper, into the storerooms beneath cold marble floors. In the darkness I am the holiest of men. When I sleep, I am awakened by blood from the feet of statues dripping across my eyes.

I am never bored. I entertain myself. I put deadly spiders along my thigh, and they inject me with God. At times, I pretend I am a man in order to laugh.

Past midnight, when the doors have been barricaded for night, I ascend and steal water from the baptismal fount to drink. For nourishment, I eat what moves across the floor in the darkness. I have never seen my food.

What need have I for companionship? Without trying, I have made an alliance with angels: my will and capability are one. And, against my will at first, I was given comrades in Hell. It is why I dance.

The saints know who I am. Because I dance, they have made clear that they may offer me no aid. Yet, they have vowed their respect for me nonetheless.

At night, to keep my body well, I climb these church walls within. For footholds I use the reliefs of Christ on his way to Calvary, as he weeps into a veil. Sometimes, as a great feast day approaches, workmen use scaffolds to polish the facades. They ascend all the way to the rotunda ceiling. It is my only sky. I choke on the dead reliquary air of a hundred years. I will be here on this scaffold, like an owl, for a hundred more. Looking down, it is again the day of my birth. And I kiss the painted blue. I touch the painted stars.

Teeth Marks

Tonight, in a codeine dream, I watched my father meet his own edges. He and my mother were standing in the kitchen doorway, beneath a vine of plastic grapes which my father had brought home seven years ago from the bar he tends. It had not been touched by any device for cleaning in all those years; there was a thin yellowed layer of dust covering the light green "fruit." Some benign blue light reflected off the linoleum floor and up their bare, painfully white legs. It accented the varicose veins across my father's calves; it reminded me of the display of sailor's knots in my Boy Scout Manual. I studied them years ago, and after being tested I would receive a small emblem, shaped like a wolf's paw, to sew across the pocket of my uniform. I was watching them from the living room floor, looking upward through my brother's legs. He was fat, and eighteen years of age. I was consistently thin with a thyroid condition, and two years younger. When the first raised voice was heard, my brother made for his drum in the corner. He slung it over his back and took the emergency stairwell up to the roof, where he had some masks out drying along the clotheslines. I heard my name and moved closer.

It was coming down. My mother was castigating him for some teeth marks forming crooked half-ass crosses on his nape. His vices were ever increasing, she was going on; he was pissing away my brother's crack at Harvard Law on the cockfights. She was bitching, as well, about him tapping too often into the goods down at the old tavern. He was half-loaded now, in fact . . . I could always tell by the greenish blotches of bile beneath his collar. She then made some reference, in sharply hushed tones, to his "putting the spiders to his jugular" with ever-increasing frequency. I didn't know exactly what she meant; she was pointing to three small punctures on the side of his neck, caked with dried blood, more blue than red in color. I thought back for a moment. I did recall one time catching him off guard in the bathroom tapping the sides of a small metal box with carrying handle and holes on the side, like the kind Oriental women use to transport their prize crickets. He was whispering some words I could not understand. I was about seven years old; he yelled at me for not knocking before entering a room and hastily shoved the box and whatever was in it out the window, where I heard it smash five flights below. He then wrapped himself in his largest fur and notified me he was going to get some fresh air. I looked in the alley beneath the window the next morning before going to school. I found nothing . . . I remember the old Irish woman who lived on the ground floor watching me from behind her window curtain with a look of horror on her face.

Reaching France

When I reach France, every promise will be kept. I want to be there, nodding in a chair from some bygone court in the hotel lobbies, with its back so high and its velvet arms. I'll sit beneath the sweet chandeliers and reflect my dreams off them, and they'll give it all back. Across the cathedrals of Paris the sun is bending, weary like the eyes of their marble saints, who blow cracked trumpets to the water birds at dawn.

I dropped out of school for sounds like that. I left it to those whose senses took the borders for granted. Who let their eyes be covered with the dull loose tissue of their dying fathers. Whose hearts did not make vows that marked those veins above my wrists for a lifetime. Left me here to pay the price which is a thin red poison that does nothing but lower the odds for my shot at love eternal. But keep your eye on me now, because I'll break each vow open, like a book that has lied to me . . . I'll leave it back where I found it in the streets for some other clever white boy to carry away.

Then I will never love these gifted whores again. Or think twice to stop and watch down a long corridor two old couples dancing slowly before dawn without once changing the music. I'll have enough money to confuse myself and I'll clutter my desk and rooms with empty boxes, and my lover's neck with jewels that whisper. Our children will come to us one evening near some ocean, with no regrets.

For now I lift up time at its edges and divide the day into quarters. When I am alone in this chair, I feel them dissolve like the darkness in a room before I take my aim. There are women with glasses and neat pleated skirts in a single row along the wall passing a baby through each other's arms. There are voices that aid me like a father, comfort me like a sister. Until the light shifts, and they crawl back to that dim alcove . . . saviors left unrecognized by heaven and its pedantic systems. Dressed neatly, with hair combed back straight. Do you know them? Do you know the place where I saw them last? Where the words have finally waited, and light in their eyes. And it's not France.

In the Law Library

I am sitting in the thin red glow of a library filled with texts on the law. The students have glasses to their lips. A tall black woman in a gospel gown is moving through the crowd with a silver tray extended before her. The tray is empty . . . yet, each student stops her, demanding more. In unison they turn to the mirrors lining the walls; their dull, loose skin turns cold and slides to their feet like silk scarves. On a revolving platform in the center of the room, one is standing describing the hardships of his youth. But he is over that now, he claims, and ready to ream any solid offer. He exposes his cock, and it is quite big. On it is the tattoo of a vault. But in the mirror it gives off no reflection. My sister is alone in the corner. She ignores the walls and uses the boy on the platform as a mirror. There she assembles her various parts. But she is sad. The last image has begun to fade. And there are no changes left.

There are few windows, and each of them is sealed. Outside, the sounds that hold morning with the wind are blue across the ice. A single bird is waiting along the line, like a small block of darkness left behind by night. Inside, some workmen are rushing to cover the windows with more mirrors. They face other mirrors. The mirrors are full. The bird is gone.

In the Capital

I come from another age, and in my dreams I meet with presidents and their daughters on my own terms. What do they make of the nearness of my features? The father seems more tired than most, dead blood hanging beneath his eyes like rotting grapes. On his index finger is a green ring that gives off signals. With a wave of his hand he commands the air, and it responds by blowing back his daughter's long dark hair for passing photographers. She's got something in a tweed shoulder bag, and it won't stay still. She whispers to me and I walk away, then I come back with much more than before and take her down. The lawn is wet and glistening black in places like perfect onyx. She tells me it is the dried black semen of the general from Chile who had visited last week. "He met with my father over lunch and talked about some shipments," she said. "Then he went off and blew up his ambassador and a grey limo . . . and that's no dream, motherfucker." I liked her. When I came, I went. I watched her father growing smaller as he waved from behind a gate.

In the fracture of dawn in the capital of Washington, I gather ticks from the ears of patient dogs on the steps of the Supreme Court. It is raining a deep rain, it blocks the morning light as it tries to enter. I see women rush by with bracelets around their ankles with pearls the size of golf balls. They smile at me. What do they make of the nearness of my features? One has snagged her anklet on a hydrant, and the pearls are scattered across the sidewalk. I'm sitting on the steps of some tomblike memorial to a man I have never heard of. I take one of the pearls up with my boots and roll it back and forth between my legs against the cool, fine marble. A woman whose ankles are bare takes my wrist lightly and leads me inside the memorial, past columns of steel painted black. Beneath an unkempt glass rotunda there is a statue, half man-half fish. The woman leans her tongue to my ear: "It is strange, but that is natural . . . the sculptor was a man who left behind nothing with his death but this fractured memory from a mind which was very mediocre and very overpaid. We are, after all, 'in the capital.' "

Stepping out of M.O.M.A.

I was a blonde along Fifty-third Street with a red bandanna pulled tight to hold back my hair. I wanted to be pure. Women from another class approach me with their dresses raised to prove to me the sheerness of their stockings. They smile. They do not smile because they are happy; they smile because they are clever. In the late afternoon, at 5:15 p.m., people left the massive glass office buildings and the bells began. It happens each day. I want to know them all, I want to come to understand them, but not one face leaves a clue. Only those who want me reveal themselves, so I must make myself wanted by each. Those who pass by too quickly for my eyes to reach, I follow. I trail them to the steps of the subway station across from the loading platform and ask if I may borrow their diary for the night.

I know this city will die before the fall of evening. I lean against a slick cool marble cornerstone with my shirt undone and my blue eyes sinking like wet lips down the shoulders of women. It is what I do each day, though I know neither they nor I will be doing it tomorrow. The others knew it as well . . . women in thin shrouds fingered rosaries and mumbled vague chants of purification. Construction workers in steel hats formed lines from confessionals to street corners. Still, they deny me my last access. I throw aside my bandanna and let my hair roll across the lips of women who have prostrated themselves to the hollow flux. Out of bitterness I walk down to the cathedral.

I was pure, sitting along the steps. Then, with the changing of wind and music, I stood and watched its shadows take the horizon. I knew what this was and what it meant, but I could not make it to the drugstore in time. With the white heat, I dropped across the fender of a halted limousine. Some tried to outrun their screams, the smart ones went down. And, right beside me, I noticed the mother of a girl I had once loved so badly. She wore a string of pearls around her neck, and, noticing me, she smiled . . . she tore apart the necklace and poured the pearls down my throat and her own. I felt pure; I placed my swollen tongue to her lips. Neither of us had come this far to die with strangers.

Days

I.

I meet my sister just before dawn beneath a pale statue on
Columbus Circle and we take the "A" train uptown to its last
stop. It is always cold and drizzling slightly at the end of each
and every subway line of New York City. There are processions passing of old Irish women returning from night with
shopping carts on small wheels, filled with lye wrapped in
damp newspapers. Their coats are too thin for winter and split
at the edges as they pull across the sidewalks like flags
dragged back from some battle lost. They chant indolently to
the leaving of darkness, then scatter into any doorway as the
sun breaks its first lines over the great wall where two rivers
meet. We have coffee in a restaurant filled with Greek workers, walk two blocks and turn through a doorway, drink a vial
of codeine solution each before ascending five flights in the
dark elevator. We were born in this building . . . and raised.
Rising, we hear the sound of waves crashing against the elevator doors and ceiling.

We visit our mother four times a year, always on the same
days . . . as if to delineate clearly for her the passing seasons.
We enter with our keys rather than ringing the bell. Her legs
are crippled . . . they no longer work . . . and she is bound to
bed. A nurse comes each day but she has not yet arrived.
That is our purpose in coming so early. She is awake as we
enter her room, which was once ours, sitting up in bed read-
ing through the instructions to a stained glass hobby kit she
had received last week in the mail.

The bed our mother lay in was constructed on her own orders. It rose so high off the bedroom floor that my sister, who
is nearly six feet tall, barely had to bend over as she kissed
the old woman's powdered cheeks. There was a small steplad-
der within reach to one side, and both sides were secured, a
few inches above the mattress, with two steel bars. "It is in
case of another seizure," she explained, anticipating a question we probably would not have asked anyway. "After the
last one I lay cringing along the floor with both wrists abso-
lutely shattered for close to six hours before that damn spic

nurse arrived and dragged me back up. Can you imagine, they sent me a Puerto Rican girl? It wasn't even one of the light-skinned ones. That was from that first agency, the one that you hired, Meg," she spoke, glaring at my sister, "I never thought I'd be thrown from some claptrap bed when I was young and rode to first place in the summer rodeo near your great-grandmother's swamp house in South Jersey . . . do you know I dream of those rodeos more than any other time of my youth? That says a lot, you know, for there were so many splendid things I did in those years. I was a beauty, like you, Meg . . . One summer, the year before your father and I were married, I believe it was, I was named Miss Greenwood Lake. It was a real resort back then too . . . not that acre of piss it was last time I saw it, where college kids go to get drunk—puking, no-class drunk, I mean—over the Easter break. You still have that picture of me with my hair down to the waist, don't you, my son? The one where you said I looked like Saint Veronica? Wasn't she the one that wiped the sweat from the face of Christ on his way to the mountain of the skull to die, leaving his image on her veil? That Puerto Rican nurse would know which one she was. She swore she was a regular reference catalog on saints!" I nodded back to her as she closed her eyes to sleep . . . yes, I think that's who Veronica was, though I never remember comparing her to that ancient photo of the old woman on the bed before me. Yet, she was beautiful and, yes, I still have the photograph some-where in the green album at home.

Our mother was deep asleep now, exhausted by the words spoken on her youth. Her head was raised up by seven varie-gated pillows, the top one covered by a satin case, the others with some cheap fabric, each of them with the name of a New Jersey resort motel labeled in the corner. I thought she looked sort of strained in the neck this way, so I slipped five of the pillows out from the bottom of the stack. She opened her eyes a second, said nothing, and fell back off to sleep. There was a cat dozing as well on the mattress directly beside her head, his tail resting across her throat. The cat was twenty-three years old. He was so fat, he looked more like an owl. For the past four years, I had never once seen him with his eyes opened. From the day I brought him home from the cellar of the old apartment on Seventeenth Street, he knew he had found a home. Now he refused to let go. Somehow he continues to breathe. I spoke to him once; he had nothing to say.

My sister and I looked into each other's eyes. She took my hand in hers and raised it to her parted lips and began to circle the crevice of each finger slowly with her tongue. When she stopped a moment, breathing deep, I followed her eyes to a picture on the wall above the bedboard. It was the two of us, ages fourteen and twelve. "God, we looked more alike than we do now," she whispered, "we wasted a lot of time back then in the room we shared together." I pulled down her hand and led her out the door of our mother's room. "Let's go see how that room looks now that we're smarter about things like time."

The room had not changed much. When we woke, I wiped something from her bottom lip and searched my own with my tongue. "From the way the day is going," she spoke, a little too loud for the moment, "you would think it was no different than any other time we came to visit her." And we both knew she was right. We hurried getting ourselves ready and back to the other bedroom. Mother was still asleep, the cat had not moved its tail. I took up one of the pillows I had removed earlier. In the corner in thin red script it read, "Bermuda Palms Motel, Atlantic Beach, N.J." I turned around the cat so that its owlish cheek lay aside my mother's. I lowered the pillow to the place and pressed down, softly, yet tight enough so that the veins on my forearm rose as if summoned by the needle. As I held it there I looked up toward my sister. Her lips were half parted and her eyes stared at the picture above the bedboard. "You know, Christmas isn't that far off," she muttered. "That photo would have made a wonderful card to send our friends."

II.

We took a cab straight to the airport; sister didn't move her
head from my shoulder all the way to San Francisco. The limousine we had called ahead for was there in line behind two
others. We could tell it was ours by the cross within the circle
painted on the side. The back seat was purple velvet, the
floor covered with eucalyptus leaves. As we moved along the
freeway with the wind through the open window the scent
carried us back to when we were young, home from school
with colds in winter after weekends riding down hills near our
cousins' home in New Jersey on pieces of linoleum after some
bigger boys had taken away our sleds. Our aunt would rub
some medicine, warmed with boiling water, across our chests.
The leaves on the floor of the big black Cadillac now smelled
the same as that rub. I reached down my sister's blouse and
cupped my hand, with its palm filled with spit and crushed
eucalyptus, over her breast. She turned her eyes and smiled.
"I remember," she said.

The driver made a turn off the freeway a few minutes after
we had crossed the Golden Gate, heading for the ocean. The
driver was a black woman, nearly six feet tall. She was
eager to please, the cross within the circle painted on her
sharp cheekbones was fading from the day's heat as she
turned her head to inform us how much time was left. "Have
they cleared off the beach?" I inquired. She told us that they
had. She formed her words by bouncing her tongue off the
roof of her mouth and the hollow of her cheeks, like a ball,
and each syllable was clear and precise. Not only did she say
what we had wanted to hear, she seemed to say it in exactly
the manner we wanted to hear it as well. "She's delightful,"
my sister whispered, "I knew mother was wrong about that
agency."

I had never driven on a road like this one. There were
many curves, and around each some jelly-fish substance
seemed to move up and down along the two yellow lines di-
viding the lanes. In the opposite lane, leading back to the

city, the chant continued from the speakers assembled across the platforms of large, speeding trucks. At last we reached the base of the mountain's far end. The driver rolled casually through the streets of a small oceanfront town. Darkness was just settling over the firehouse. It was the tallest building in sight, and the siren-shaped speaker on the roof played on the deep chant. Some workers in tight wool trousers were returning home from the chapel near the redwood grove, their wives trailed with sickly infants straddled around their necks. Prayer beads, the size of cranberries, were fastened to their belts with plain wooden clothespins. The driver turned to us and spoke, "These are a very independent people, we offered much money to keep them off the streets this evening but it is *novena* time and they would not listen . . . the beach, however, will be cleared as promised . . . we are nearing it now, in fact . . . this would be a good time for you to sign the register." She held before us with her long fingers a large book, bound with barblike wire and covered in suede. A pen inside marked the place for my sister and myself to sign. We then turned the page and, in the blank space following, added the proper remarks. The car engine stopped. We sat at the top of a twenty-five-foot ramp, leading directly to an empty beach below. The Pacific Ocean was at high tide, so that the waves swept a full five feet beyond the base of the ramp. I looked at my sister. She held out her hand for mine.

The driver stepped outside and spoke to a genteel old man with soft grey hair. He was dressed in a tweed three-piece suit and, at one point, laughed casually at a remark the tall black woman had made. The meeting lasted only a few moments; she handed him the suede-bound register and returned to her seat behind the wheel. She said nothing more. Two young women in plain tan skirts and no top clothing to cover their large breasts opened the doors beside my sister and me and proceeded to bind our hands with silk stems and place thick strips of fur across our eyes. They asked about our comfort and withdrew. We could hear the gravel move under their feet and the sound of a car door slammed shut as they began

57

a conversation on the beauty of the light across the upper ridges of the mountain at this time of evening. The driver began the engine. I could feel my sister's breath leaning closer to my ear: "We have waited too long before moving into eternity." We felt the car plunge forward.

As we heard the waves plunge through the four open windows, the fur was released from our eyes, the stems were freed from our wrists. We watched the driver dissolve behind the wheel like a mannequin in a pool of acid . . . only her two eyes remained, shaped like glass almonds; they rose with the clear green water to the roof of the car and set there, frozen, fixed down on us with an ominous detachment. I took my sister's hand, now I would never let it go. We would glide forever. She smiled. Her eyes filled with a surfaceless light. I tried to lead her by the hand out the window. We could glide.

But I was wrong. The desires inside our dreams are not fulfilled therein. I saw in her eyes she too had realized it, just before the crosscurrent swept in. It slashed my fingers in hers, cold and quick like a frozen knife. She was being pulled away, out the window and at my left. The fast water pushed my screams back into my lungs, I was being pulled away . . . in another direction. Always and forever, in another direction. . . . I wanted to let go, but somehow I continued to breathe.

And each dream is of distance. I move like a shark, never sleeping and never ending, and always an equal three feet and no more from the milky azure floor. I touch nothing, and nothing will touch me. My speed is always the same. It is neither fast nor slow. It is the speed of some aging thief, stolen himself by the tide. I hear constantly a chant of unyielding distance. I do not age. My eyes pump upward some strange dull light. What I speak is pressed back inside before the words are formed, so there is no longer a language by which I can think. The only thought is distance.

And it is the same for her. The same speed, the same distance from the ocean floor, the same thought, the same dream. She circles the earth in another direction. And once a year we pass each other, on that date that marks our act together. Even for that moment the dream does not change, of distance. And we do not touch, although our hands are forever extended. Even the light pumped upward from our eyes does not meet; it runs parallel, instead, to the surface, raised by distance into the sky.

The Transient

They were the cheap rooms on that floor, with the bathrooms
down the hall. Late at night, through his insomnia, he
counted the times the women used their shared toilet, espe-
cially the giggly pair in the room two doors down. They were
young; they'd been there only two days. One always seemed
to take an awfully long time, much too long to simply urinate,
even taking into account, as he did, the possibility that they
were drinking California wine throughout the night. "She is
maturbating; it is obvious." He said this, for some reason, out
loud, and realizing what he had done, realizing that he might
easily be overheard by one of the passing women, he wrote
out a note on yellow paper. It said, in block letters, "Talk
silently to yourself," and he attached it with some tape to the
frame of the mirror. He returned to the image he held of her
(it seemed unbalanced . . . tentative and precarious). This
time he kept silent, however. Maybe that was why it slid
back and forth. She was rubbing her clitoris in circles with the
tips of her pinky and thumb pressed together. She was cooing
very softly. Again, he mimicked this imagined sound, ab-
ruptly, a sort of glottal strut, out loud, then quickly checked
himself, peering up to the mirror and shaking his head . . .
these things were difficult. Lacking any imagination, she
thought of nothing in particular as she manipulated herself . . . only of the narcissistic pink color of the door before
her. (He knew the color, having used the ladies' room himself
when no one was around.) The expanse of pink opened out
in her mind to a meadow of blinding pink light, pink as the
clitoris she now rubbed (her fingers pressed together in a
triangle, like some oriental greeting).

   He always used the more clinical choice of words in his
inner dialogues, like "clitoris" or "penis" . . . never resorting
to those vulgar euphemisms. He thought words used in their
formality were much sexier. He heard these words spoken always in a voice not quite his own . . . an assured, command-
ing female voice . . . that of a wealthy child's guardian, or,
more specifically, the voice of that one woman doctor on the
staff of the ward he had occupied those three Christmases

ago, the doctor he always asked to have his sessions with, but was never allowed, forced to see the Chinaman instead.

She was returned now to her room, her roommate having answered the squirrel-like knock, and they were giggling again as if she had never left. "God, the doors here are thin," he thought, "can they hear me when I sing along with the radio?" He panicked at this notion. Resolved NEVER to do THAT again, never to sing out loud. He drew another piece of stationery from the drawer and wrote out a reminder which he again taped to the mirror, this time to the bottom of the frame. It read, "Thin door . . . don't sing either . . . ever . . . but inside is O.K."

He heard the girls' voices louder now. He didn't mind that. He enjoyed hearing them, though he wondered what there was to laugh about constantly. Then he thought . . . no, he was certain . . . that he could distinctly hear a man's voice among the two girls'. Suddenly their giggling annoyed him incredibly. He felt it as a physical force, like a branch snapped in his face by some wholly inconsiderate stranger passing before him, single-file, through a thin trail in a woods which he suddenly recalled. Like a cuffing across his frost-stung ears by a nun as he arrived late on a winter morning. The giggling no longer seemed airy and expansive, trailing out into nothing but the hallway. It seemed now stifling . . . tightly enclosed and claustrophobic, moving directly into his brain . . . into the small room which was *his*, which *he* had rented (at daily rates). Now all their silly, childish laughter was only in response to the deep voice of a male he pictured, obscenely between them, lying back on the single bed's spread with the same orange and brown pattern as his own.

He was surely dark, this fellow, his belt was unfastened and, apparently, he didn't care. His bass voice seemed to curl like a jungle trellis or snake around objects and tighten itself there. At this moment it was fastening itself around the girls' wrists. He was waiting, hoping, in fact, that they would scream for help, yet they only continued with their ridiculous giggling. He felt a swift anxiety and rage . . . the smooth

walls of his room were appearing to crack into wet stone
blocks, as in a cell. He tried an anxiety-reducing breathing ex-
ercise which the black nurse on the midnight-to-eight shift
had taught him. It involved breathing through alternate nostrils, but he couldn't remember which nostril to begin with
and that, as he recalled, was all-important. The walls were
dripping . . . he tried beginning with the left nostril. It
seemed to work. The walls began to look smooth again. He
felt the plaster. It was smooth . . . nice.

He was about to call the desk to complain, but he thought
better of it. He was mindful of another nurse he favored back
there telling him that they had great difficulty placing him in
this hotel, and not to cause any trouble . . . to be as inconspicuous as possible. He jumped up and made another, smaller
sign in block letters, taping it beside the others on the mirror.
It read, "Be inconspicuous."

Already standing, he headed to the washbasin. He preferred that term to the word "sink," it was listed that way in
the hotel's brochure which they had sent him: SINGLE
ROOMS, INCLUDES WASHBASIN, ADEQUATE BATH-
ROOM, BATHING, AND SHOWER FACILITIES IN
HALL (he liked the word "facility"). He began to run the
hot water. It was very hot; he could brew tea in the morning
or prepare instant coffee with water run hard, directly from
the tap. The rising heat fogged up the mirror of the medicine
cabinet above the basin. Then, as if to prove a natural, God-
given advantage over the giggling girls who, by a necessity to
squat, need use the toilet down the hall, he proceeded to piss
directly into the flow of water, watching a spiral jetty of wax-
thin yellow circle the drain and disappear . . . the steam forming droplets on his penis. When he was through, zippering
back up his pants, he looked up into the mirror. In the fog
formed in the glass there from the vapors' ascent he, without
realizing or intending to (so that it somewhat shocked him),
had written plainly, "Have found the only advantage of being
a man."

Just Visiting

When the shooting broke, I decided to vault the teller's window and face the fire from the other side. They saw my forearm tightening across the throat of the cashier, Ms. Lattimore, and as my Browning was raised to her temple's pulse, they took it back. It all fell dead; with the silence I felt the distance between my trigger and the man. I heard the reverberation of the last stray bullet's muffled ring; it moved out through my brain in circles of jagged light expanding like still water broken by a stone. Some smart lieutenant arrived to take things over. He leaned his eyes a moment through the doors, then went around back to throw the switch. The light rolled out of thin vapor tubes above me from right to left. The darkness absorbed more silence. I could hear their details being assigned. The tone of the head man's voice was clear: they were hot to blow me away. I didn't expect my hostage would go down as a deal, I knew she signed *that* paper when she took the job . . . but I just wanted some last contact. I would have rather some sweet clever music. I slit the strap to her bra I reached under I felt my palm rinse her breast. It could have been a radio. I moved my lips closer so only she could hear me. It should have been a radio.

Whispering, I told her, "You see, all my life the women I have been with . . . and that's more than you could imagine, really . . . I always bypassed their breasts I went down, you know, I went to the source I honestly don't think you're going to die so don't be afraid, listen . . . I wanted the thunder on my fingers, on my lips. What are a woman's breasts? Just so much adornment . . . they lie like some chalice on an altar waiting for adoration. Like the writing on the scroll . . . the handles on the urn . . . the gold that lines the vessel. I wanted the mystery inside. The thunder and the darkest light. I mean, I feel the sharpness of your nipple, it is flawless, no doubt about that, just let me move it over here, oh, it came out . . . it's so red. You must be younger than you appear . . . I know about that kind of thing, really. Once I told

this girl she had breasts like bleeding lemons, she thought
that was a beautiful thing to say. But what are they? . . .
just architecture, where is the wetness? And why are they so
white, so terribly white? Whiteness frightens me horribly.
When I was fourteen years old, I went to my friend's house at
the beach in Long Island. The sun there on the sand, I remember it, it was terrible . . . too much whiteness. I couldn't
stand it I stayed in my friend's room for days and listened to
music. His mother and his fat sister thought me quite insane.
I wanted to teach myself to play the drums. The sister was
thirty-six years old and so fat, the mother had to tie the laces
of her shoes. I hated her and she hated me, but I was just
visiting so it wasn't very fair. One day I bolted out of the
bathroom while she was listening, leaning up to the door and
I jammed a pencil into her jaw. She ran away crying about
lead poisoning, but you know, you really can't get lead poisoning that way, it's a wives' tale. I know about these things,
really. At night, when the shadows cancelled the blinding
white, I'd go down to the beach and run because it is important to keep the body well. That's in case they ever come
again. You, I'm sure, don't concern yourself much worrying
about them, do you? You know, your breasts are like that
beach, so white and dry . . . yet so near to the source . . .
the water and the motion of the waves . . . what could ever be
more pure? Please allow me to just feel down here . . .
I won't try to sneak anything up the wrong hole I know that
can hurt if you're not used to it. They did it to me. I let them
think I didn't really care but I found a closet down at the
end of the tier and I hid in it and learned things and made
marks on my forearm with a fork I snuck from the cafeteria.
You can see here, the scars. It's not just an X, it's actually an image
of the cross Saint Peter died on. They nailed him to it inverted,
he's my patron saint. Ahhh . . . there it is . . . and wet . . .
from fear? Wetness is not whiteness but so dark. Whiteness
is the color of death, you know, not black. Wetness

is life, the breeder and shaper of life. In the beginning the sun was black. So all light was absorbed before it had a chance to return. And our dreams, then, were empty."

New York City Variations

Noiselessly, the world has begun to defect.

New lampposts curve over the avenue
in darkness, like chrome tears.
In sunlight, drops of android sperm
frozen above traffic, loud and green. I live
on an island where I was raised, flanked
by rivers. To the east, great bridges.
To the west, tunnels. Palisades. Sunsets changed.

This bridge an old, sinking web,
the trapped scales of a saxophone
Struggling to set themselves free.
They will fall one day, sink small ships
passing beneath with the weight accumulated
over years. Carbon dioxide and ice. Crystals
from poisoned towers. Hats and veils from war
widows, crossing for Easter. 1949. 1951. Fragments
of hydrogen bombs, dark from the Pacific. Screams
from jumpers, released from Bellevue, like spiders, returning
the night I was born, to claim prey in midair.

The moss under your fingernails it feeds
on the sweat of my lips. I remember that.
It was summer the ships were towed back to port.
Uptown the yellow taxi pulled away leaving your hair
to dry in the wind. I have been living beneath the streets
under the sharp blue light of subway wheels. I know the
    streets above.

My training ended at twenty-three years of age.
There was nothing left but the mountain of the sacred
    maiden.
And you. You with weeping wrists and your chaste forehead.
who drove all night to meet the sun
in the eyes of ascending gulls, gulls who haunt my poems
like hands of apostles in the sky.

I have walked these streets so often I could
forge the shadows of skyscrapers as they fall
to rest below the sculptured air of midtown.

Air-conditioned blood drips like rosaries
from glassy facades to the cosmopolitan eyes

The fantasies of secretaries are washed to the streets
or trampled beneath thick heels along subway platforms.

Engineers in orange helmets point out the flawlessness
of buildings which do not yet exist. My hands

drain with boredom or lust. It was time
for evening in Times Square. There the dim-witted clouds
at once unbuttoned, revealing a nasty aperture beneath
    thin blue cables.

I stored daylight in secret attics
since I fell in love with guns,

my youth sealed in vaults crowded
with an infant's idea of Heaven.

Night rising straight and fatal as a vacant syringe.
Seven times it fell in blocks, immediate as a bloodstained
    image.

We had pride in our bodies . . . they moved
with the sureness of death across cathedral walls

Our coats hugged us slick as the sharkskin air
And in our jeans we dreamt of Times Square empty at dawn.

Concealing weapons, we crashed under boardwalks
near ocean's amusement park and in the sky its stars

blew some riffs lightly.

My body has been perforated
with a strange idleness. From it chaos
flows like blood trailing an abcess,
the poison itself long since passed.

Precision, I build this altar
to you. For what was taken
from me, I need

A competent God to praise,
to raise me above
new cities, whose climate
is grace. Still
gardens of winter. A bell.

Thick veins on the back of my forearm,
like the rope of an acrobat,
have risen again

As a line of demarcation
between fields of battle
which vacillate easily but with some small pain
across this flux of anguish between light and dark

past and future   ash and flowering flame.

What matter for thick armchairs and fine shelves for books?
I chose apartments for loose floorboards to hide the secret.

On Fifth Street the bell at the window summoned children to
    classes.
Toward night the sirens emerged. I mastered the raging of
    birds
Rising through floodlights. I collapsed across the black sheets
And ripped open my back on the fingers of dried sperm.

Voices from a red radio come down,
pin me to this bed as if many
iron bars were sealed against my wrists.

There is an owl outside this window.
It follows me through Manhattan, persistent as the blocks
of sunlight at dawn. And there are cities.

I was born and surrendered in the city
and it has made a difference . . .
when I hear the owl I think of stones.

It comes through the window
as if the balance might be restored.
And I sing because the long wait has ended
And raise the floorboards where under the sinking
of an eyelid like a blue vault sleeplessness sits with folded
    arms.

Here I walked with a memory of workers in midtown
returning at day's end to safe edges of home near water

Streets abandoned to a purer grace, until the summit
of tall buildings is where the light of evening sleeps

And in the slit shadow below, blasting my way
through the taxied vapor, I finger the turbine mist

I wait on the origin of night's sounds waking, I know
that here only the blind man sings, even in rain

The notes of drenched violins turn like warped mirrors
and the last cloud parts slowly, like a cracked wheel.

It seems I have misplaced the directions for childhood.
The maps laid across my veins are changed by sick night.

Outside the women form rings
that neither sing nor dance
but chant to an angel in white gloves
whose eyes speak fever and dissolution.

Yet in my room   Youth charts its distance.
The fragments of my rage descend   like a moth
from this ceiling to lie across the quilted evening
Smashed tentacles of inertia,   I am trying

To abide by rulings. The half-fulfilled dream aside,
I walk here dangerously across ice or stone
With nails in my boots like a lame stallion.
Dogs came to my hand and spit to seal
the punctures in my forearm and I am again
a part of the condition   of man
by the grace of their tongues.

Back to the streets always, ravaged and wet,
strained with midtown exhaustion, late afternoon
when the clever walkers funnel the wind of taxis
or shift to the sky to peel wet words from their eyelids.

The strangers with slick hair are wont
to strangle schoolgirls at these mirrored hours.
And the shadowed edges are worn and light is towed
by buses and the nod is shattered in the sheer height
of federal buildings further down. I watch this island
where I too was born and spent my youth walking, not
    waking.

Walking on grey on green in Central Park I wore
slit jeans and a shirt from Jamaica blue and yellow
with a hood and many red buttons I did not own it.

Some detectives in worn suits slide at my door.
They told me Eddie was dead on Lexington and 103

stabbed in the jugular at mid-day
outside two automated hospital doors.

He often walked East Harlem after dark, high
on reds, calling out the black man. Before the sheet
   descended

on his eyes he grabbed the nurse's wrist
to check the blood was real, he signed one last paper

to donate properly his eyes.

And I salute you, my brother.

My needs were few and pure.
I swept powder through the green shafts and sought
to understand the grace in death on subway toilets.

I took the time to lie
in barber chairs in lobbies of ruined hotels
and breathe antiseptics surrounded by mirrors.

I drowned my own eyes and surfaced
to jars of combs in varied sizes
like strips of human brain preserved for a woman of substance
who waits across the lobby on sofas of crushed red velvet
guarded by shadows bought by years without sunlight.

At eighteen years of age,
Sad on the ridge of Upper Manhattan
under the Cloisters' Spanish shadow
I wanted my blood to wash clean the Palisades.

I came close to binding myself within a stolen tapestry
to drop from the rail of the George Washington Bridge
and shatter against the drifting condoms
that float like dead eels across the Hudson by dawn.

In midtown again the way you stop
casually to finger your hair
in some grey drugstore window
across Fifty-third Street the Museum of Modern Art,
that poverty vault.

I fell right through the deep there once.
I felt the light of Nolde scratch beneath my fingernails
and I found poverty once more.

So much poverty. It follows me through subway cars.
Poverty to die a death within one's own family.
Poverty of the darkness across the ice. Poverty of cataract
    eyes.
Poverty of young men alone behind the stairway, who practice
alchemy inside bottle caps, who know
the altruism of a last syringe.

I watched a street gang heading
at me on East 106th, their hands
touched the pavement as they walked.

Tired of cheap revolvers and exploding fingers
they came to understand the beauty of the knife

And I ran. I clutched the twin scorpion in my crotch.
I was thirteen years of age I was pretty I was white.

Marked by a more distant sky, I hold
a black sponge to flush darkness
in the thin canals of night
between midtown buildings.

In this city.
In this century.

I squeeze it above my head
to rinse my eyes.
when I am tortured by women passing
more beautiful than the unnamed flowers
that bloom in the dreams of children
dying of fever.

In another century.
In another city.

Children more fluid than gardens
Unveiled in some future desert
beyond the shift
sleepless with thirst and memory
far from the city. The cities are dead.

A place more brillant than women,
or the scream of the earth's own sun. Or
dark, then, as this moment returns, a loneliness
which rests tonight, greets me at dawn
with its cruel, smashed fingers.

I drank cough syrup in alcoves
of vast men's rooms in Grand Central Station.
The eyes of broken commuters leaned
against me like tender knives.

And I took trains
to wealthy suburbs to walk their streets
and summon up clap from queenly town daughters.

I settled in Rye at midnight
walking until dawn, the tall reeds
near the cemetery were fingers
that beckoned me to lay.

And with the sun I set
on the graves of soldiers dead from the Revolution
and understood there the hilarity of fear.

Not surprisingly
I lost track of the seasons
writing biographies of the haunters
of my dreams in infected urine.

As if time had been mine
to blast anyone away
in the stare of my ambition.

Check the way
the gargoyled facades are dissolving
in the hot breath of tubercular doves
over Duffy Square when the sirens ring at noon.

Then Christmas on earth will burn in this city.
The furnished rooms, just down the street,
are filled with flaming white hair . . .

and I must go now and assume this responsibility.

California Variations

Like a rabid goat, this obsession
runs crazed
Until the desire itself
is broken and wasted
beneath the weight of its hooves.

The torn clover leaks and slides
beneath it. Some greater flower
evolves from the strain.
The suffering relives its past.
The echo recedes to a former voice
and the canyons which carried it upward,
To passing birds, close in their walls.

On the cliff
I cover my dream
with fallen tents
that held them in sleep,
the sleep of pale quivering eyes,

the canvas marked by angry teeth
like the skin of seals. I carry them off,

bury them with precision or flames.

I rest with the dogs across the feathers of birds
    departed for winter.

I hear thinly colored dew forming beside me, eyes vacant
in the stupor of redwood fog . . .
sweat and shattered hair down my forehead
like boneless fingers of children back home.

Distant, alone without language or fear

as if I were among those wounded at war
left across an open courtyard
in a village far from Paris or Milan

hearing the small voices of women in love.

I'm walking, the sleep for a time has been left behind.

In the moist process of my dreams I sense
the far planets grown plutonium slick.

I crush the agate beneath my feet where lice, swollen
tender as the nipples of women cursed by blood, drift

across the red tide, they use drowned offspring
to bridge the shattered reef to shoreline.

Why can't the phantoms stay silent in my dream
until I have mastered the laser behind my eyes?

I am trying to abide by the clues
in the dreams left half-fulfilled,
on the deathbed of each brother,
where the tears of a sister stained the milk-white sheets.

And I look to my generation
and dream in blasts of hydrogen,

where the residue of all my nights
is changed to stars.

The process is a circle, is brillant and works,
as the final collapse of dying suns cradles new ones to life.

What is this force that continues
   driving me to such clothed desire?

It binds the angel's fingers with the strings of mute violins
to close off the light that rises from their crevice,

breaking time into fragments of sound, like teeth grinding
in the distance, I must search for an instrument to pierce
   the thread.

Then I follow, as light settles across trees for evening,
   Breaking through.

At night when the wind is slow my dreams
they tangle me in red nets beneath bridges
where water does not flow it chains my eyes
to the sliding clover it locks pain between
my hungry teeth to feed on dissolution without grace.

I know there are trapped doors beneath me
as I walk, whose edges are sharp with light
I am willing to fall because I feel the power
of each shadow within it   A stunned purity
and grace where the angles of sleep are flawless
and a kind of oblivion straps its thighs across my ribs.

There is so much invested in the shields
and wired fingers circling the edge
the way gravity reverses time
at the rim of a black hole in space.

You must return to find the faces obscured
and the future becomes a past filled
with hideous, nameless angels and their familiars
whose lips are tight and split by milky fingers.

Some recent memories of love return, they hesitate
only in sunlight . . . like a hand fixed for violence

longing for blood beneath flesh.   It's horrible
when you come to know what you thought to be
the end was only a postponement,   to come back rushing,
Rushing covertly, tired at night like an aging thief.

No longer does the dream register on waking
the way blood blossoms like mercury through the neck
   of a syringe.   No longer the body pressed
Damply against your sleeping flesh,   night growing
   between your thighs.   How faintly each star recedes.

This transient sun begs to me, walking down dirt roads,
to summon somewhere a face by which it might
reflect the purest light
before the clouds reassign the angles.

I cannot control the distance of the shadow,
though when birds rise, I watch.

If some careless lovers make plans beneath my window
I do my best to overhear. Outside my window
The lines of evening are staggered along the hill like beacons.

Horses.

Standing blank and dumb, cold,
close to numb in the end, like
a dragon's paw, at the edge the moon pressed
tighter, until it is reduced over and over
into the point of a needle . . . like Cleopatra's,
an obelisk to fear within uncertainty,
reflecting onto the shields mounted beside him.

He did not jump.
he has, in his mind,
jumped so many times
before he wonders perhaps

he has already
jumped. But he knows
I am thinking
In my mind as well he has
Jumped so often.

I am alone. I am
alone until one
hits bottom faceup silent or dead.

I feel the roots, dry as desert snakes,
choke my liver until the urine screams
as it flows into racks of glass tubes
hung from the bedpost. Why am I still here?

Now from my nostrils only dead branches grow.
These are the words of a man who poisoned
his own faith. Who made the tree a leper,
where no season begins or ends. Vanity. Pride.

A heart, once wild,
now half
devoured

How much time has been wasted, waiting on benches
in the greying of light near water?   When the vine
embraces your calves like a clever lizard   and the eyelids
Are lifted by maggots in dead sand and the scent
of piss stings the color of smashed opal? But it will end

because the blood continues to pump
with an inexorable vanity   and the crude heart
cannot sidestep the faint persuasions of grace.

Before I could try it I was handed the mail.
It comes in neat packets, secured by ribbons,
a cruel joke for one who has waited so long. . . .

Why is it sunlight brings us the day's sad news?
So these words form a crevice, and the language
slips through. What difference does it make?   My memory
has been shattered. The smaller each fragment the more
I am obsessed by numbers. I write the numbers on paper
and hold them to the sun, waiting on its reply.

The distance, then, is horrible.   But I can wait.

But this righteousness expands constantly
like music straining to finally mix with light.
The volume increases until each decibel stings
and the auditorium is bare, except for you and the magician.
                    Who never reached the stage.

Of the rest, many still gather in the streets outside.
This is a valid alternative, and there seems to be
among each a new trust for the other
as if they had uncovered, as one, some terrible hoax.

But I call you coward nonetheless . . .
for now the magician too has departed,
and you have left me starved for an evening's entertainment.

And for that I had waited so long.

The possibilities of this blindness release me.
The sun rears and, with subdued rage, turns back.

Beneath it divers crash
like rubber sails abandoned to the reef.

I hear the whale pass northward
across the swollen white on their hands
shaped like bat wings and their wounds filled
with turquoise and blood. We are still as they dive
and dutiful gulls snatch this fur from our eyes
                    to patch their wounds.

The fur is still thick across my eyes. I feel
the angels' breath beneath me, split by the shields.

But the passing of the wind guides me to the cliffs
until tides begin to shift, and the vapor rising
is radiated within. It seals the scum against my teeth.

I press my lips to blocks of stone. My tongue
tastes the shivering moss, soft and black like wings of crow.
Somehow its weight has measured the distance I have
    traveled.

The clouds this morning are low and broken.
There is a gravity between us that longs to seduce
wind from my heart, so the details of women passing
are obscured by the opening of light through their fingers.

A hand in a white glove runs a knife through the sand
Until each goal worth risking is tunneled with blood
And the time left to me lies blind beneath it.

Then each hour is like a thief. Its hands bind my own
with silk stems, and wrap thick fur across my eyes.
Who is the idiot within me that goes on, without the gift
of time and space? Who left the love of a woman too far
   behind
sitting on the edge of my bed, her ankles spread like flags
                       across the carpet?

It was impossible to know the fragments
would fail to join the horizon.
I was left with so many good intentions,
on the edge, without this pole for balance.

I stared at the other side, the solitude of birds
returning. Rain began to fall. The crevice would open.
I summoned the angels, they showed me tricks one might do
with an ordinary deck of cards.

They listed the visions I bargained with
and left with bleeding on cluttered sheets.

And they will reclaim them now at an incredible interest.

The distractions are tireless. The pools
Left behind by Tuesday's rain so clear.
Yet the hand reaches to touch bottom
And the light from beneath dissolves like a vague alibi.

Day after day the processions move out in dazed fragments
like stones across sleeping water. Lines of dazzling parvenus
whose eyes descend over the dust like footlights.
Debutantes with weeping tongues, their Spanish boots
surround their thighs like slick vines at roadside.
They follow in circles, though none will intersect
the point where each began . . . where the shadows form
slow crucifixions on wet sand. And I sit
On a bench overlooking the sea.

Starting with little in mind
the best you might do is take it
                all the way.

transforming the real earth
to textures turned inward beyond control.

We sit huddled in winter coats, fixed
to the logic of stones.

Locked tightly to the seams of night,
the moon reared like the fenced stallion

and, with subdued rage, turned back.
Then the hour is loose, the music

Is vapor passing through, and defies
the quick changes, as wind outdistances the word.

But the wall is high.

the black bonds that chain my eyes
to the sliding clover

for this dream must shift
and the sky is fit.

And the planets will lock
in orbits that trace the signs
to the strength of silence walking away
through the deafened ridges, blood-red for dawn.

I.

My body across the mammal green
   waking with grass between fingers
   wet like sperm.

Or unmapped desert
with many suns like suicide jewels

I am slapped across eyelids by the rude mariposa.
And at night stars crush the curtain of my lungs.

                  To sleep again.

II.

Morning's light cuts the milky quartz
   like slit photographs of you I once loved

Music the calypso of eucalyptus swept
             from snake-smooth ridges

The boy child stoning mustangs
with eyes of a trampled doll.

The girl child's shadow, walking away,
is cool like moonlight to the fevered lizard.

III.

With my companions of youth I wake
   where the diesel trains pass at noon each day.

The wind across these tracks tires my eyes.
The sunlight on cinder is grey like our youth.

Leaning on my back; salt wounds of the Hudson
            and exploding beer.

Many days the smell of drifters' burning flesh.

Chased by railroad cops, we slid through metal fences
with the quickness of diesel light on bending mirrors.

The signs, our emblems are out
of print, like a book marked
dangerous to the state. But here,
on this edge, the faceless shields
hold out. Their weight awakens
the vicious gravity. It instructs
The gathering seabirds, who check
our blind side. We are too poor
for our spirits to relax

For a single moment,
moment to moment,
each moment drains
like water into the buckling sand.

We sing
to regain
our proper rage
within the distraction of constellations
and this damp, squealing earth
which smells like the breath of a cancerous pup.

We need a more visible enemy,
a language of human will. We need
the level plain of our sister, distant Masada.

Meanwhile, think about us here.
We have a radio, a tower. In the might of those others,
find a way to reply.

Poems 1973–1985

Poem
for Frank O'Hara

My footsteps in the shallow
Ocean pools, the poisoned lips
Of the anemones set loose my eyes
To fly to the horizon, time's own memory

I see a single ship passing,
Shadowless, that one which never
Arrived, as you stood, years before,
Waiting in the harbor, dressed for love,
Your loose breasts throbbing as if beneath
Their surface small fish were feeding on your heart.

Winter's Age

Your hands are like two mirrors which press
dry the flowers so many young daughters have
chosen for the blind and the grave.

Beneath halves of walnut shells
my eyes are switched, back and forth,
in the slight fingers of a confidence man.
So for all these years I have had to cheat to see.

The red and softly frozen sky
is transformed by night on these streets
To tears without faces. Without reason.

Where are the noble tears,
tears which, fallen, from thorns
beneath the rose, the tears which convert
the frail peasant girl to a saint of roses?

Remember this: The past draws blood.
Its fingernails are cut off
on the edges of old winter skies,
forgotten and forgiven. They fall, stiff and black
Like dead hornets into the soft treetops.

For Elizabeth

It is winter, ending on earth.
The planets align tomorrow
in March, and grow more distant
from the sun and each other
like stray, worn soldiers retreating
from an enemy that no longer exists.

It is a mild spring in Purgatory.
In green Limbo the children whose foreheads are dry,
whose hands do not grow, are transformed, themselves,
to seasons, or birds circling an obelisk
of shivering mercury. None are allowed
prey. None are allowed heaven's crooked beak.
They are radiant swallows, or hummingbirds
with thorns for tongues
to feed on the shifting mercury
from the mythology of God's hand
which I cannot break, even now,
under this tearful scrutiny.
I've tried.

I am allowing to pass through me
a statement of death.
You, the catalyst of such distorted memory.

In that Limbo the children move
in some strange gravity within and
outside grace. Their Lord is angry.
They have died with their innocence untested.

None knows what they have been,
or will be. Each day it changes
without changing. Do you understand
what I am saying? It is the life you chose
on this earth. The life of junkies and lies.

But that wasn't you. I knew you.
You had perfect lips, eyes like
a true child. Your breasts unformed.

This place where I have put you now,
It is a cursed season, an awkward
line, a flawed circle. A snake on fire
devouring what, tomorrow, it will itself become.

Prologue

Starting with little in mind
the best you might do is begin it
over and over again. Transforming

the real earth to a texture and strength
beyond control. I am thinking of a wave.

We sit, huddled in winter coats, transfixed
to the logic of stars collapsing. The fresh
gravity pulling at stones we grip.

Locked tightly to the seams of night,
the moon rears like a fenced stallion,
and, its rage subdued, turns back.

Then the hour is loose as the music,
a vapor passing through. It defies
each change. As the wind outdistances
each word spoken, and replies with
a promise already broken.

M. Verdoux, The Wife Killer

My verdict has been passed.
Now the order of my judgment draws near.

With no more questions to answer,
The time heats up. Even the past
Moves swiftly. Only small detail
Draws me into the timelessness of closed walls,

Scratching the faces of my murdered wives
Into the gravel. From the fragments
Of passing clouds I formed whole bodies
Of penitent jurors, picnicking beside a lake.
At times a single cloud appeared, shaped in each detail
To a finished image . . . a dog, a terrier reclining
With tight wire hair. Then there was the tower,

Which cast the same shadow from all angles
I remember in my youth a tower was the archetype
For wisdom and endurance. The bird which circled it
For a thousand years. And yes, I study the sounds
Of the train which passes each afternoon. Late,
When the sun is dull like her eye through that strangled veil.

Now is the morning of that day.
I hear the workers in the yard and move
To my window. The guillotine rises within
A block of stray darkness, like the blade
Of a lovely skater. I hear the signal,
The switch is thrown. My priest enters
As the bars slide open in unison, like shadows
Of my former selves, many and thin and wasted,
Marching with precision toward a passionate goal.

A Night Outing
for James Schuyler

A distance beyond
Sky's reach, membrane
Of leaf a miracle
Against my elbow

Through the tunneling light
Merging deep beneath bare ponds
With the scattering tension
Of its own blueness

Reverberation

Lifting myself
Into the silence
Of rotting bark
My calves tighten
Against soft floors
Of dead pine, two elk
Trapped in the oubliette
Of your eyes' iridescence

Listen

Earth's blue grinding
Out of thick pine
And insect ballets
Rising

The way still grey water
Throws the moon,
The cautious moon,
Right back at itself.

Wing and Claw

When I dream of you this way
You are so badly with another
I can feel his breathing
Inside these sheets.
I understand the pressure of his smell
Better than my own.

This is the moment when I am totally receptive,
Calm and unthinking under a shivering duress.

I was born for these moments,
Controlling all excess,
As if I were a skillful bird
Of prey . . . taking all I want,
yet returning for more,
Having emptied my crooked beak
And claws. It feels good
To expand so fully, talon and wing, in the path
Of the full and faithless moon.

The Ad Man's Daughter

Inside these bottles
Rows of tenements are burning.

I wait here at 5 A.M.
for the homeless
to come to our door. . . .

I hear the metallic
hum of red lights turning
green on Sixth Avenue.

Not as loud as taxis, seven flights
below, fierce with speed for dawn.
At this hour you can hear anything

It's 2 A.M. there, in N.Y.C.
where you are sleeping or awake
inside the sound of waves. The strangled wind
holds light across the bedroom window, then cuts
loose its sound, a whip that shows both ends.

Saint Theresa

Her tiny heart
pierced on a thorn
heats the jealous rose above it.

The thin stem of dried blood
spill from her palm
one by one together
like a locket from an envelope, a gift,
which soothes her Lord's unkept promises
without malice or regret. Only

a great vision remains, it uproots
The numb vines
From your clasped fist and whispered psalm.

It falls like the silence, its leaves
turned light in the purpose of your genuflection.

In Four Seasons

The seasons are a series of transparencies.
Slowly, slowly in your eyes they are aligned,
In your hand overlap. You have given up

So much grace to a fear of changing storms,
Each one's mystery requiring such different provisions,

A set of improvisations. Like the phrasing of slow,
Half-forgotten songs. To that fear you have given up your
   youth.

Winter, you saw no purity in the stillborn snow.
The landscape meant nothing to you,
Only its quick decay in your flushed fevered palm.

Summer, the sun was a relic, a coin uncovered
From some volcano's ruin. Its heat
Opened the pores of a grave which arrived by mail
As a gift in spring. And fall,

You wore that casually, a sweater fastened loosely
Around your waist. Always in case the cold arrived.
You prepared yourself for the most superfluous orders
                    of the earth and sky.

It was only those days of transformation . . . the few
Yet tempestuous In-betweens . . .
Which were gripped tightly in your hand
Like a divorced ring

Which you finally managed to remove,
Uncertain of what came next,
Though it was only the remnant
Of a failure you would never give up.

Wedding in White

Your bride came naked. It was sad.
In my eyes she passed the shops with cameras
And swan-necked lamps, and, raising
Her head back with a small question,
Tasted the bone sweet rain. Tested it,
Like a litmus strip, with the purple
Turning of her tongue.

Young, inelegant, honest,
Her bridesmaids followed.
With their weak memories and hard-pressed lips,
Followed her every move. The crowd stood wet
On the steps of a cardboard gazebo.
It was a strange sound, at my feet,
Of rain across gravel, like a drum with tight snares.

To have each desire met
If only for a day
Seems a fair thing to ask
Since you promised to obey.

Dead Salamander's Song

The sistine eye,
The twisted thigh. If
Dead skin says nothing,
Then it cannot lie. But

Its coral breath
Could light night when alive.
And its will to outsmart
the sun was a dance
Which no language survives.

Ghost Town

Without death to understand
The tomb is shut down,
Like a well that serves
A whole community, their well oiled
Hearts already exposed

By a thirst for something else outside their reach.

Soon no one is left
To measure the dust with sunlight
To wipe the stains
Of crushed fuchsias
From the coastal road. Or record
the cries of treetops stung
By salt spray through the mesa wind.

To time the marathon
Of spiders invading abandoned
Webs inside pumpkins rotting on their vines.

Only students pass through,
Looting warm beer; burning
Rocking chairs left on the beach
Crabs tumble back into the slick

And miles off a lighthouse
keeper, stranded for mail and fruit
From shore, smiles through a telescope

With a great vanity.

Painting by Flashlight

In a temporary room
Walls a strained yellow
Like a Japanese wrist.
Lexington below lights out,
I light a flashlight against
Utrillo. A weightless snow in
The upward strokes, that is,
The bleak branches
Thin as torn fingernails.

There is a sense
Of danger, to study a painting
With a focused beam, surrounded
By the transient darkness of hotel rooms.
As if you were a thief examining
The numbers of a safe. You step closer,

The grey building's facade
Scraped with knives from
Madmen, perhaps, fleeing music. Mauve
Bonnets on the shoeless peasant girls,

Intense as bag ladies outside at this hour
Uptown, weighing the possibilities
Of streets intersecting. But these girls

Walk in numbers, hand in hand, toward
A farther, deeper perspective. Out

And through these walls.
As the batteries burn.

Bad Signs

I.

We are still farther from that star
To the left of the Trump Tower
Than we hoped to imagine. Here
On Fifth Avenue. It never moves,
Though it does recede.

II.

We are nothing
Whose only certainty is
We are in something's way.

Heroes

for Phil Ochs

Fallen one, your private ghosts are
stepping on you from the heights
where you left them off. Their necks are
tiered like a noose. But we don't need
that. Each eye sees a different tattoo. . . .
You changed my life. I sat in the rain
with *The New York Times* to get your act down.

Now you move
through these crowds
knowing the indulgences
Of each maneuver

like a needle
through the satin that lines
the restoration of an old, old crown.

Poem

Asleep in the corner bed, her breath
climbed diagonal, like a bent cat
across a slanting roof. Her supine eyes

hollow and dull in the glare
of a standing moon, as if a candle
held above her face had tipped slightly

letting drip there two thin
pools of violet wax. The other features stolen,
as if seen on a screen where the subtitles
flashed constantly, ripping the attention.

Everyone chose to follow the dialogue . . .
hardly noticed the tight flesh
of her cheeks, begging for the fingers
of a stranger. The screen went silent.

And she was alone with the camera
closing in, leaving large her urgent lips,

like pale questions.

Nightclubbing

For this generation,
infected with too many antidotes,
there must be a balcony, a height
where one may be lifted up
beyond the timorous grip of glamour,
of glory without rage,

to initiate and incite the shaded dancers
who are eager and anorexic, wearing
monkey teeth on their wrists,
lips or fingers painted black,
passing out affinity with the howling dog
And their trousseau of darts,
As the letters of their tattoos dissolve,
Leaving mermaids and flowers, the banded hearts
Stranded without vows or names. . . .

I challenge you to restore
a reckless elegance in place of
The vapors you breathe of hubris and boring
saturations of such civilized distraction . . .
to commit to sleep in a painless chamber
The tedious pets of your cradled syringes.

I can license you
the malnourished but willing
innocence of a cloudless destiny
And petition you to summon the mysteries,
With joy not envy, dissevering the crooked
Braces you insist on wearing, without blinding
You with too much at once, the forgotten elements . . .
I'm talking about a very slow first move, and carefully,

as you reach, as I reach too,
Through a wheel of thorns
To pump new air into the stray rose.

Post-Modernism

I gather up the giant holes.
Why should I bother with the rock
and sand which fills them?

Why should I bother with distracting weights
Without elegance, or allow myself to be taken
hostage, leaving only through back doors,
a gun raised to the pulse of my lucid shadow?

The Rites of Arctic Passage

Shifting shape
to an adaptable species,
they abandoned me.

Their compasses dive into the frozen waste,
sensing home. They explode in the thrill
of their own exactitude. The imagination
empties itself. Turns blue. Blue as the expanse
which clings like the shadow of slow bombers.
Blue as the poles' shivering horizon, so near

in each direction, where tribes, breast-fed for life,
gather to worship the auroras of solar wind. It enters
here like thieves through a warped skylight, finding
Nothing but a bridge table and 9 future almanac

aside a hooded corpse, who drifts motionless
outside laws of man, nature, and reason. Fingers
chinking like glass birds on a windy terrace.
Eyelids like the claws of a bear. The white bear
that watches me now, knowing the terms of sacrifice,
understanding on behalf of what I have become and
pretend to be.

The Caves

I am part of these walls.
The cool moss is a calendar
to my ancient dreaming. These walls
were painted by the cycles of the moon
passing through the bodies of women.

The true signs are faded. All that remains
are the parodies of heaven, all that remain
are the bison and stag, a briefing for the hunt,

an inventory. Yet night and the fire
can reinvent the screams. Tracing my hands
across the veins of fury. Gripping the bone
of a generation which was shaped by its child
into the head of an arrow.

Judging the Pageant

The sun splits into two
like a futurist eye.
You may have your choice of either.
I'll take what's left.
You know my indifference
That's why I was chosen. Now watch:

One sets west
this evening on a line
where the ocean departs, serious
And loose, a flamingo bending to feed
from the cupped palm of the horizon.

The sun set east
like a jealous twin
This evening: another horizon, rigid
And dense, a coin stuck halfway
In the slot of a glass tank. Remember . . .

the coin's on fire,

And your choice is final.
No matter to me.
All I want is your reason. Between the two,
all I care for is the difference.

El Hombre del Ombre

Take the letter "H" from a Spanish
man on the streets of Madrid
in his native tongue

And that man will become
a shadow among the French.

Suspicions

I.

The sun grew
Over the watering can.

I licked its shadow
Later, descending
On ice.

On ice I remembered
my brother's will

and the consequences
of a pain, kept dormant . . .
as if frozen so rapidly.
Its own source, like a river, was lost
Or forgotten.   I forget
things at times.

On ice
I hold the shadow's hand
As it skates on by.

II.

A madonna
With the partial tapestry
Spilt wine
And split candle.   Is a dream

with nothing left to steal.
The real world lies to itself
to be real. The quality
Of their life created by the passion
Of their lies.

That is the only way
for them. Threats mean nothing

to them.   They seek the formula
for flawless strangulation.
Their coats are wide, and buttoned with care.

The assassins buy tickets over the counter
and no passports need
be forged again, in time.

III.

The barricades have attached themselves
to every waking moment, every movement
I make. My memory, as well. My will,
last night, led off to the station.
The barricades of History have secured
Augustine in some dark grotto. I used
to see him in sunlight, as I read, pensive
on a sitting rock streaked with dull lines
Of opal which he refused to polish. It would
have dazzled, pushed the sunlight across the
eager grass surrounding him. Now no saint to evoke
with his taut changing features dreams between
his written words. No small talk in the brush strokes
Of the works which that night Van Gogh burned in the
   meadow. . . .

IV.

Is she, in the seclusion of her strained wealth,
so finely rehearsed, is she proud of heart?

What would redeem her?
It *is* true; she has tried

in her room, where the paper on the walls
is changed each night

like her mother's necklace, she dreams
of letters burning slowly in her dresser

and with her guarded fingers examines
the markings on her skin, swollen less
than she wished, and blue   as dead flowers
kept pressed between the pages of a stolen book.

Where did they come from, how
were they made when each night
she sits at home, leads herself
early to bed, alone in the darkness
inhaling the smoke, which has been burning
for years now, the words sealed tight with ribbon.

Late some nights her mother enters.
In whispers she remarks to herself
how flawless her daughter's skin
in the light of the thin moon which
Enters nervously through the windows,
Flanking right and left the supine dreams.

Her mother departs
caressing the paper on the wall
as she sweeps closed the door,
her long mauve fingernails clicking
Against the wood, like rodents above
Seeking shelter.   She has woken.

And she will sleep no longer this night.
It happens often.   She is not afraid,

only, at times, in doubt. There is,
She is certain, someone, something
within the walls of this room.

She was raised in wealth
And she has never learned to hide.

Sophia

Disgraced by sleep, she wanders
long corridors
of a countryside in white,
tight and bent, a spent candle.

She circles the edge
of the field with dawn,
cursing the twilight breath
the valerian scent the dreamless
immensity. She screams,
fearing the distant
mountain has split the sun
which she has made a vault
for her mistrust, and the statuary
erected by intimidation
in her name. At her will.

And she waits, and walks
until it fills itself with
the whispered promise, directly
above. She grasps its phases
inside a mirror, as if she could
halt the progression of its arc.
As if she at last understood
the meaning of its silence,
maintained within the wake and rage
of solar wind, the shrinking, devious
gravity of distant dwarves.

And losing it all to the western sky,
She steadies a magnifying glass
Before her breast, burning open
The abcess of her heart, releasing
that wisdom and that shame.

A Window in Cherry Valley

Across the pond
reeds bow against
the soft charge of night

change

further down
they are fingers
inviting me to the pleasures
of death by water

Its split-second
passion, its surrendered
sound of exploding lungs

like poor bells ringing
underwater and
it's late at night

On Tour

Each night another room
without changing, the white
walls grow less bright, like
color returning to the joints
of a hand that feared flying
but no longer cared.

It comes with a Bible and
a print of Paris under grey
winter, women walking in couples
toward a monument that endures,
room to room. Night to night,
the faces of the women grow closer.
I am trying to read their lips.
Give me a week and I'll succeed.
And I'll regret having done it.
For now I make out a single word
and a name . . . "Caesar Augustus"
and "abattoir."

Aside from this
There is little else. . . .
I get in late
And sleep until someone calls.

Then I go, leaving everything
As it was . . . a bed, a bright-
colored chair. Perhaps a desk.

It's like a poem.
The smaller the room
The neater it must be
Once you're done with it.

Dueling the Monkey

for Lou and Sylvia Reed

The fair lady works at shuttles
Brush knee and twist step
Play the lute
Part the wild horse's mane

Golden cock stands on one leg
Watch with fist under elbow
Lift hand
Insert needle to sea bottom

Step back and repulse monkey
Flash the arms (unfurl the fan)
Separate your instep
Left and right

Stork spreads wings
Turn and strike with heel
Paint the bottled fly
Strike tiger left and right

Turn around and cast away your fist and palm
Blow ears
Dodge and kick
Sweep lotus with a single hand

Step forward to form seven stars
Press face with vanquished palm
Brush knee and underbelly
Stand back, deflect, parry, and punch

Cross form and ride stork
Step back, seeming close-up
Lift hand
Embrace tiger and return to mountain.

A Child Growing Up with the Sun

The sun sits back, watches the street
like an informant for the junta.
By now, I understand each motive
in the sky, and its shadows on earth.

I am helpless nonetheless. It's tough
when an immense power cannot be terrorized.
When it is invulnerable to a slip of madness.

I acknowledge its brilliance, as I was left, by choice
to shadows. And in that shelter, I dreamt.
I spent my youth's desires like a peculiar currency.
It was a running joke between myselves,
the one I believed in, and each of the others.

It confessed its innocence to me
through Mayakovsky's poem. Once,
It poisoned my skin in the Rockaways
to get my attention. I took it for granted.

That was a magnificent mistake.

I never learned to trust it. I wore dark
glasses, disguised my skin in hats with wide brims.
It knew too much, its vantage points always
too well chosen. Where did it go at night?
thought the child, and who did it meet and what, exactly,
did it have to report? So they grew, these suspicions,
as one. And I chose, instead, the dark dance of the moon.
In the face of two, I have always sought the lesser majesty.

For John Donne

Stars, in their unchecked lust,
ejaculate still onto the barren moons
their pulsating milk. The solar winds

like Aurora seeds, enter
At the poles of this planet, above and below.

Don't you see
the obscenity of glaciers, waiting like
aged dictators, blinding white,
impatient for their cycle to devour?

Born of this,
we watch night grow,
voyeurs of cloudless nights,
impatient and pathetic
to imitate its pleasures, to uncover

the code of its birth.

Eugene, Oregon

for Judith and Aeron

The promise
Within a cloud . . . Rain?
Small gods in jealous turmoil?
Scale? Hypnosis?

Rain,
I hope. Then
I'll find the plum

leaves across the sidewalks,
Small, crescent and wet

To peel cautiously
Up as they press
The pavement like forged labels
from bottles of pills
To sleep outside the law.

Like scaled decals
For a child's serious
model airplane or ship,

Like flags to signal
Danger from the bridge
In high water, our engines gone.

Borders

I.

The border patrol leaves shut the gate,
Orange and black. Along the bottom a spider
begins another web. Got thousands. The gate
never opens. Guards just check for circumcisions.
Siesta in booths. The radio on . . .
radio on, One corner lit orange with coils
of electric heat that melt the fallen statue Madonna de Mount
   Carmel
into a greenish pool of radium glow
until a fat sergeant grinds his heel into it
as he signs forms for the capitol, molding
it into the threads of his leather jack-sole,
into the shape of submission. With the radio on.

II.

On 96th and Park walks she they call Chameleon.
Crossing the street her Puerto Rican eyes and skin,
like smashed glass buried in clay, transform in daylight, in color and shape. She turns downtown,
a matron in white skin and fur, the doorman hands
her mail, the many invitations she will never attend
all those future nights, when she turns uptown,
crosses 96th like an immigrant, her borderline
her almond eyes. No one had forgotten her lips.

The Novena Tide

They are old, in black
stockings like suicide nets
And breath, days-old from varnished lungs,
Like sealed corridors.

The sweat of their vows
radiates in the cracked marble
like the spit of ikons.

The mercenary flames of candles
hatch promises like eggs. The shadows
shiver and escape, like serpents
from the frescoes of Genesis.

See the tears across the veil
in the glass-stained light?
Like salt dew across the virgin
web of spiders, protected by whispers
And thorns. God makes pacts with His predators.

See how loudly these women
Pray for sons lost inside another language?

Our Desires

There is a wind that seeks the crevice
under my heart
the way insects file at night
beneath a doorway

Its edges are rough, it slits
the cords. It trips my steady breathing.
When it comes there is no one
I can trust.

It seems, at times, I have designed
too well this vision of you.
I cannot survive your eyes
when they are scarred with a need
for some lesser form of love.

I admit to this conceit.
And though you will not accept it
You love it nonetheless

It is just like you. Our desires
will always be kept sharp
by a kind of perversity. A need
to be each forever alone. . . .

Its color is violet, like lips
that have been smashed by night
or robbed of blood by lack of breath.
The wind I was speaking of does this.

I can feel it now.

My Debt

for V.S.

I come to your bedroom door.
I come slowly, and alone. A scented wind
Pins me. It seems ominous, but I'm not sure.
It is as if a document were posted there
In some obscure language, revealing all and nothing.

I need to cry out,
Loud and anonymous,
Off the crumbling walls of Western night . . .
If I could disguise my scream
Like a distant jackal beneath uncertain moons
I could ride awhile on time alone.
It is my right.

But the tribe of this language,
Of these words, is finished.
It is the long cry, now, of the dead.

A ghost be my translator . . . but the ghosts
Owe me nothing. I have no justice here.
I am asking for too much.

But I did come to your door.
I came slowly and alone.

Letter to Sister

Young woman, you are about to fall.

A vague thunder in the basin
of a thousand mornings . . . children
pasting the fermented dream on walls of cheap linoleum,

The tension of wires across your eyelids,
light like aluminum chains

in the shadows
as you turn, young girl

about to give?
About to?

Painting cheap dogma across the text:
"A room of one's own"
in the mirror . . .
oak-lined mirror,

printing death mascara
like lines of demarcation
across your lead raven eyes.

In the oak-rot mirror,
powder to face like dust to dust,
you'll return
these cosmetic ashes of reptile bone.

Steep in documents
of astrology and fear

fingers raw from searching files
of nostalgia libraries and
in the waxing floor, dreams
of accomplices and father's misfortune.

About to recall?

Under the diaries . . . feverish dust
among patent leather . . . shivering lies
shelved above the closet's green ruins
of the cakes and bracelets they have presented you . . .
living in a city of barred windows.

In the service of TV sex
and Mexican beer . . .
your idea of failure a breast
untouched by tears.

Radio afternoons spent in terry-cloth robes
caked with sweet, noble vomit of infants.
The legs heavy with thorazine and varicose,
thick like purple vines across your calves.

You will take classes one night a week
in the new poetics at nearby community colleges

initiating the final curse. . . .

About to move?
My sister,
about to?

Then you slide under a moon of horrible breath
and sick flower.

Then you rise.

On Susan's Birthday

Brown woman with watermarked eyes
lay beside me on polished teakwood

That's all I remember of the city . . .

Spanish boots choke her thighs
like slick vines, a Roman nose
that breathes only the scent of burning orange
her eyes drip like bleeding almonds

A passion for excessive detail
leans like a crucifix between her breasts

She skims her fingers up my cheek softly
like stones across sleeping water

This is where I reach her
not in the flame but in the pool
of a wet dream always and just after dawn

when the sunlight hesitating
at the window

is a shadow outdone by the purer light
pumped upward between your thighs

Poem

It's sad this vision required
    such height.
I'd have preferred to be down
With the others
    in the stadium.

They know the terror of birds.

I am left, instead, with the deep
    drone . . .
The urgency to deliver light, at least
    a fragment, as if it

Were news from the far galaxies.

Across America

A pavilion of clear voices,
a fused brightness revealed
Without joy, temptations of vertigo
among the tenants of the rosary.

This spirit rests in vacuums of chrome.
It fills with the scent of a dying sun.
Inside this place we recall the names
of rivers extinct for the oceans they might fill.

The shade of roses, their fabled grace
Swept from the ledge, by which we enter what passes
With our hands to breathe this perfume
which cuts like a smashed machine.

How say you to the air-born promise, twice concealed
to my memory? Your son's courage is grand
and manifests along a straight line.
It communicates with such exquisite fever.

This love combats itself, delaying
the assemblage of a final frame.
Sober, absorbed and disfigured . . .
preserved now by the bolting of carbines.

Dresden to Chesapeake Bay

The train sits airtight
beneath the Chesapeake Bay.
The nets are rising above.
Again he dreams the Dresden dream

Of her, surfacing
from a basement filled with the skin
of oranges, wet and loose beneath the shattered
pipes. She climbs the wooden stairs, in a borrowed gown

and he follows
down streets, each lonelier
Than the one before.

There are no flames, only wheels,
detached and rolling,
a vicious red route through smoke
faster than the panting
of cheetahs breathing to the scent,
tracking deer flesh. She surfaces

far and near,
sooner or later, destination unclear.
He hears through the engine
Of his plane the curve
of another terrible horizon, guilty
For not yet being born.

This Spanish Town

The children are playing
in your ears, old man, your ears
like heels of clay from the arena
of the bull.
Your eyes, old man,
like bronze nails dug
from the boot of a dead matador.

This Spanish town
where mosquitoes hunt
in the jammed aqueducts
whose white columns are bloated
like the bodies of the border guards.

Once there were whispers
and wings in your dreams, pacing
the streets like a hawk who flew
low as the eyes behind cracked shutters.

one flight up. Now you sleep
beneath a child's hat, the shadows
Only of burnt bottles
Beneath you on this street each evening.

Red in dark ashes
Like the eyes
Of the daughter sent
To bring you home
Again tonight.

In the Deep Green Vase

The petals of a soft yellow rose
speak urgently, as if they were labels
sewn by fierce young girls, held captive,
with the suture of their wounds.

Here in Ward number six,
in the corridor in the deep
green vase, grows another rose,
younger and more subtle in its cautious bloom.

Its irony is the way it has strained
To achieve the sublime.

Perhaps it is like me.
Perhaps it is afraid of light
and dreaming by day.

Its color is that of the lips
of a young mute girl
they allowed to return
home for winter, her hands
still at work, stitching day and night.
This, her final season, her finished desire
distributing the contraband of roses
smuggled from the deep green vase.

Poem

I snatch a grape from her breast
as a drunk steals apples
he will never eat.

In a dark room
the eyes of tearful birds glow

and it is cold there
your breasts shrink like nerves exposed
to the whisper of spiders hanging
from fixtures of attic light.

Seferis knows this place
and his ancestors
whose faces are dented
by the wind of mythology.

How often can a man be rebuilt?
For my part, I feel petals of zinc
clogging my pores.

You would appear better off,
hair mixing with sunlight on sand,
but you wear a longing for death
tightly across your forehead
like the mask of a surgeon.

In pools that sing on the mountain of sleeping maidens
I party with the ghosts of my heritage.
Some sing in German, some sing the song of Druids,
they do not recognize me, and they do not care . . .
they will feed my flames to the cold winds of night.

For Ebbe Borregaard

I.

I see it passing
in silicon deserts.

It cannot slow down
though, at times
I will gather enough speed

to fix my motion
onto its tracks

and gather its eyes
like dice
into my fist

to weigh the vision there
against my own.

II.

Its power to deceive
can burn or freeze,

Can easily slip away.

It studies its maneuvers
in my own eyes.

It charges itself
in my strength.

As I tighten the grip

It throws me, broken,
into the dancing chaparral

to choke me with chaste laughter,
and presses my lips deep

into the dreams of ants feasting.

III.

Found it once more in the ocean's rush

Laying myself convicted
in moon-spiked surf,

Coasting foam and salt spray
ripping the ear deep,

I hear the death clock ticking there like dried bones.

It handles the darkness well
and smashes it across my ribs like a gull's scream.

It clings to torn fingers
like fetus flesh.

I want to fling it deep
into tides of lunar madness

But it rides these waves clean
like a flawless surfer

And dances a new death
across the stones . . .

where I summon the rays which cry from the crevice.

The Runners

I.

You hear the call,
the struggle of winter.

I watch the shapes of shade
which run from children
like frightened birds, children

who crossed the line of peculiar night
without warning, or proper humility.

II.

Their voice, as one, was heavy
like words flung across a swamp.

Then the voices broke, overlapped
and ran. As the swamp began to run,
becoming a stream, clear and dangerous.

III.

Thick as milk from a peasant's breast,
gravity presses them to this floor,
a carpet of moss and stone. Then they think
with a painful clarity, the clarity
of a heretic's flames.

IV.

Here, every lost act,
no matter how distant in the mind,
ends in murder.

3 Short Poems

Poem

Some trust the wolf
they have raised since birth
not to turn on them.

Some trust their lives
In the hands whose fingers
Are five silent knives.

Some will be reminded
of nothing, or perish
By that memory.

Compassion

Stepfather, I wanted
to spit in your mouth
as you lay in that casket,
to put beneath your tongue

some drops of the moisture
which you scream for this moment
in the piles of hell.

Cinco del Mayo

I live in these hills, made heavy
   with tanks, their tracks
    Leave pools where small, round fish
    Like coins with wings swim as if
    In the footprints of thunder. Here

Every day is Cinco del Mayo.
Everywhere is the Equator. Every hour,

motionless above women and men, the sun
watches or waits like a god or a threat.

Things That Fly

I.

My blond niece speaks in riddles
to her uncaged bird

Like Francis of Assisi and his flock
of wolves, a shining mist at dawn descends
like a wall to words between them.

II.

Misery may be folded
in half, like a sheet
of blank paper. Or filled
With words. No matter.
It is only a first step.

You must continue the folds, parallel
To each side, until their intricacy
builds on itself, forms a delicate
grace. Separate. Facing itself.

In Japan, there are beautiful words
For each step. This way misery dies

in equal parts, until it forms
a paper missile at twelve noon
to fling out any window, without
aiming. But only from a great height.

For Robert Smithson

A hummingbird, slow through the camera,
drinks fame from the blistered hand of a tower

In midtown Manhattan. In Mojave, desert flowers
grind their teeth for midday.
Between the breathless flags
Of the canyon, only the tumors
Survive. Only the cracked skull
of cattle, their shadows perfect

triangles. You told me one night,
only the most casual humor
fit when you were drunk at Max's. Out there,
only the spiral stones, laid out in serious
colors, like the crossing of ghostly tribes . . .

arranged like the letters of some lost language
on the jetty. How perfect your last
Vision of them from above, a part

of the air there, too light for your wings.

Borges Death Mask

We become the children
Of a dream that recurs over time.

The lips of the mask
Were white as the finished flame
Of fire in some concentric ruins,

Its eyes pale red
like the tongue of
A caged white bear.

Its features were simple,
the drawings of children left alone
To live along the blacktop of a schoolyard,

shaded like those
whose final will
initiates our dreams.

I call them father.
I wear a mask.

The Desert Casino

I pour water slowly
into the fragile vase of your lungs.
The seeds burst upward
from your heart. You are an extravagance.
Flowers push

finally, by morning
through the black soil
of your breath,
out of your lips.

Never stop. Never. Now

I put on you, like a gaudy cape,
long, long sleep.
You dream in German. I answer
with the sound of scissors sharpening.

It is becoming too much for me, this life
around the desert casino. I throw buckets
of sterile buds
of mariposa
blood-lilies
into the pavilions of cacti and mirrors
at dawn. I sit,

a salamander on the hood
of a pale blue Chevrolet
in outraged heat, tired of the obsessions

for passion, and the small, sleek ornament of risk.

The jagged pieces
Of last night's games lie
Across the checkered sand with
The shattered teeth of coyote.

Music Television

The cable rises
up the midtown
Building's facade like vines
ascending virgin trees above
the hills of Fatima, the grotto
at Lourdes. The wires are attached

with great care, the last
module inserted delicately
like the final stone in an altar,
that one anointed, filled with relics
of saints, delivered in vast
European processions. Finally

the knob is turned. Music
arrives before the image
appears. Only a moment,
confusing to the faithful,

And the screen glows
like X-rays, revealing
the bones of some martyr's
shriveled fingers, then a blond
woman in stripes, then a living
hand, painted blue . . . everyone's
watching. It seems to be working.

What could I have been thinking of,
saying
what I said?

Sleeplessness

Without sleep, without dreaming,
How can I break you down?

Is it sympathy or envy
That causes me to wait up, bedside
With a pale, anorexic moon?

I wake you; cover your eyes
With postage stamps painted with owls
For the commemoration of insomnia.

I have come to accept, in these hours,
The rules of an efficient terror. In these hours,
Which repeat nightly the same precision,
Which are louder than the rest. The sound of
These clocks like birds across a tin lawn.
The cat smashing his paw against the TV
Screen, as a missile arcs across the background
Of a flag. The station "signing off."
Just like me.

In the Gears

Of the jungle
In the desecration of the iris
In bloom for images juxtaposed
In the quasar mist, the mitre
Of white dwarves, the bishop's claw
In the conclave of authority
Among straining stars

I abjure all velocity as I shatter
Each commitment, the words in vanished gold
inlaid in walls like Mexican teeth.

In the birdcage beneath my ribs
In the panic of the hummingbird
As it swallows my heart
Through the sly thorn of its beak

In the compromise of the clock
In the hour hand's folding
Across seconds like trapped ells

In the harmless crystal made
Mad on your lips, sewn by decay
And night, in the emblem
Of pedants with exploding luggage
and gauges for elegance,
In the subscription of hearts
In the strangled teeth of work
In the judgment of each word
In the end, pretend you hear me.